S0-EKL-049

CUTTING DOWN THE ODDS

There were two Arapahos on top of the girl, as Skye Fargo raced his Ovaro onward. He got within a dozen yards of them before they saw him. The one pulling at the girl's skirt leapt to his feet and yanked a tomahawk from the waist of his breechclout.

Fargo reached down to the narrow holster around his calf and drew the double-edged throwing knife known as an Arkansas toothpick. Bending low in the saddle he threw the balanced blade underhand. As the brave spun and dived to his right the knife slammed into his side and buried itself to the hilt.

The other brave got to his feet and drew a jagged elkbone knife from his waistband. That was fine with Skye. It was the way he liked it, one-on-one, winner take all. . . .

∅ SIGNET WESTERNS BY JON SHARPE   (0451)

RIDE THE WILD TRAIL

- ☐ THE TRAILSMAN #49: THE SWAMP SLAYERS   (140516—$2.75)
- ☐ THE TRAILSMAN #51: SIOUX CAPTIVE   (141660—$2.75)
- ☐ THE TRAILSMAN #52: POSSE FROM HELL   (142349—$2.75)
- ☐ THE TRAILSMAN #53: LONGHORN GUNS   (142640—$2.75)
- ☐ THE TRAILSMAN #54: KILLER CLAN   (143086—$2.75)
- ☐ THE TRAILSMAN #55: THEIF RIVER SHOWDOWN   (143906—$2.75)
- ☐ THE TRAILSMAN #56: GUNS OF HUNGRY HORSE   (144430—$2.75)
- ☐ THE TRAILSMAN #57: FORTUNE RIDERS   (144945—$2.75)
- ☐ THE TRAILSMAN #58: SLAUGHTER EXPRESS   (145240—$2.75)
- ☐ THE TRAILSMAN #59: THUNDERHAWK   (145739—$2.75)
- ☐ THE TRAILSMAN #60: THE WAYWARD LASSIE   (146174—$2.75)
- ☐ THE TRAILSMAN #61: BULLET CARAVAN   (146573—$2.75)
- ☐ THE TRAILSMAN #62: HORSETHIEF CROSSING   (147146—$2.75)
- ☐ THE TRAILSMAN #63: STAGECOACH TO HELL   (147510—$2.75)
- ☐ THE TRAILSMAN #64: FARGO'S WOMAN   (147855—$2.75)
- ☐ THE TRAILSMAN #65: RIVER KILL   (148185—$2.75)
- ☐ THE TRAILSMAN #67: MANITOBA MARAUDERS   (148909—$2.75)
- ☐ THE TRAILSMAN #68: TRAPPER RAMPAGE   (149319—$2.75)
- ☐ THE TRAILSMAN #69: CONFEDERATE CHALLENGE   (149645—$2.75)
- ☐ THE TRAILSMAN #70: HOSTAGE ARROWS   (150120—$2.75)

Prices slightly higher in Canada

Buy them at your local bookstore or use this convenient coupon for ordering.

NEW AMERICAN LIBRARY,
P.O. Box 999, Bergenfield, New Jersey 07621

Please send me the books I have checked above. I am enclosing $_____
(please add $1.00 to this order to cover postage and handling). Send check
or money order—no cash or C.O.D.'s. Prices and numbers subject to change
without notice.

Name _____

Address_____

City_____State_____Zip Code_____
Allow 4-6 weeks for delivery.
This offer is subject to withdrawal without notice.

THE TRAILSMAN 70

HOSTAGE ARROWS

by

Jon Sharpe

A SIGNET BOOK

NEW AMERICAN LIBRARY

PUBLISHER'S NOTE

This book is a work of fiction. Names, characters, places, and incidents either are the product of the author's imagination or are used fictitiously, and any resemblance to actual persons, living or dead, events, or locales is entirely coincidental.

NAL BOOKS ARE AVAILABLE AT QUANTITY DISCOUNTS
WHEN USED TO PROMOTE PRODUCTS OR SERVICES.
FOR INFORMATION PLEASE WRITE TO PREMIUM MARKETING DIVISION,
NEW AMERICAN LIBRARY, 1633 BROADWAY,
NEW YORK, NEW YORK 10019.

Copyright © 1987 by Jon Sharpe

All rights reserved

The first chapter of this book previously appeared in *Confederate Challenge*, the sixty-ninth volume in this series.

SIGNET TRADEMARK REG. U.S. PAT. OFF. AND FOREIGN COUNTRIES
REGISTERED TRADEMARK—MARCA REGISTRADA
HECHO EN CHICAGO, U.S.A.

SIGNET, SIGNET CLASSIC, MENTOR, ONYX, PLUME, MERIDIAN
AND NAL BOOKS are published by NAL PENGUIN INC.,
1633 Broadway, New York, New York 10019

First Printing, October, 1987

1 2 3 4 5 6 7 8 9

IN THE UNITED STATES OF AMERICA

The Trailsman

Beginnings . . . they bend the tree and they mark the man. Skye Fargo was born when he was eighteen. Terror was his midwife, vengeance his first cry. Killing spawned Skye Fargo, ruthless, cold-blooded murder. Out of the acrid smoke of gunpowder still hanging in the air, he rose, cried out a promise never forgotten.

The Trailsman, they began to call him, all across the West: searcher, scout, hunter, the man who could see where others only looked, his skills for hire but not his soul, the man who lived each day to the fullest, yet trailed each tomorrow. Skye Fargo, the Trailsman, the seeker who could take the wildness of a land and the wanting of a woman and make them his own.

*1861, northern Colorado,
the Arapaho land at the foot of
Shadow Mountain where the real shadow
was the shadow of death . . .*

1

He didn't want company
He didn't expect company
He sure didn't welcome company.

He'd chosen the little hollow because it was sweet and warm and out of the way and smelled of cedar leaves. He'd tied the horses just outside at the edge of the woods and now he watched Molly Ludlum slip her blouse and skirt off to lie naked in front of him. She was as lovely as he remembered, all of a piece, a smallish girl but everything balanced, breasts, hips, legs. His lake-blue eyes moved appreciatively over her as he slid his own shirt off, undid his gunbelt, and dropped it on the star moss.

Molly reached arms up to him and her sweet breasts lifted, their small brown-pink tips already growing firm. "Fargo," she breathed. "I didn't know how much I've missed you." He smiled as he sank down atop her and felt the soft-warm sensation of flesh against flesh, sweet, sensuous touch that flooded the body with its unspoken message. He pulled his Levi's buttons open as he pressed his lips over one modest, beautifully cupped breast. He had just circled the tiny tip with his tongue when he heard the sudden, sharp sound of hoofbeats.

He drew his lips from the sweet mound and frowned as he let his ears become his eyes. One horse, he grunted silently, moving hard and fast just outside the wooden terrain. He stayed atop Molly as he listened, waiting for the hoofbeats to pass. But the frown dug deeper into his brow as he heard them veer and head straight for the hollow. His hand snapped out, yanked the big Colt from the holster on the moss beside him, and he turned as he heard the horse crash into the woods. He had the revolver raised as the horse burst into the little hollow and the rider reined to a skidding halt. Fargo's quick glance took in honey-wheat–blond hair hanging down to the shoulders, gray-blue eyes in a finely-featured face.

The girl stared at him over Molly's naked form, shocked surprise in her eyes. "Oh, my," she bit out. Fargo lowered the Colt as he saw the surprise turn into disapproving disdain. "Sorry for the interruption," she said icily. "I saw your horses."

"The sight of horses always send you crashing hell-bent into the woods, honey?" Fargo asked with irritation, and Molly pulled her blouse half over herself.

"I was looking for help. There are two wagons under Indian attack," she answered.

"Where?" Fargo asked.

"Half mile or so west of here," the girl said. "I was on high land when I saw the attack. I turned and raced away to get help."

"How many Indians?" Fargo questioned.

"Maybe thirty? I didn't stay to count," she said tartly. "Well?"

"Well, what?" Fargo grunted.

"Don't just lie there and ask questions. Get your horse. We've got to help those wagons."

"Forget it," Fargo said, and sat up. "It's all over by now."

"Maybe not. Maybe they're still holding out," the girl countered.

"Not likely," Fargo said grimly. He turned as he felt Molly's hand slide across his arm.

"You can't be sure," Molly said, and he frowned at her.

"Sure enough. Besides, you two going to take on maybe thirty braves with me?" he speared.

Molly's lips tightened and she lowered her eyes but he heard the girl's voice snap out words. "You could do something but it's plain you'd rather indulge in your own pleasures than try to help two wagons full of people," she said, contempt wrapped around each word.

"We saw a platoon of troopers riding patrol, not more than ten minutes ago," Fargo told her. "They were making a wide circle. Ride due north and you'll meet up with them. They're the kind of help you need."

The girl threw him a glare of gray-blue contempt. "Thank you for nothing. Do enjoy yourself." She whirled her horse in a tight circle and charged out of the hollow. Fargo listened to the horse race out of the trees and onto open ground and felt Molly's eyes on him.

"You can't just let her ride off alone," Molly said, reproof in her voice. "Not with a war-party on the rampage this near." He fixed her with a grim glare. "You know that's not right, Fargo," she said.

"Shit," Fargo muttered as he swung onto his side, yanked the gunbelt to him, and rose to his feet. She was right, of course, he knew, turning his back on her lovely nakedness as he strapped the gunbelt on. He swung around and pulled his shirt on and saw Molly had drawn her blouse over her dark, curly triangle.

"You wait right here till I get back, you hear me?" he ordered. "Don't you get any fool notions about riding back to town alone."

"I'll stay right here, promise," Molly said. He tossed a grim grunt at her and strode from the little hollow to where he'd left the horses. With a smooth, swift motion, he swung onto the magnificent Ovaro and sent the horse into a full gallop. He picked up the girl's tracks at once, saw that she'd followed instructions and raced her horse northward, the line of hoof marks cutting clean and deep into the ground. He sent the Ovaro racing alongside the hoofprints and silently flung an oath into the wind.

The girl's intrusion seemed but one more surprise in a week of surprises. He'd ridden into Owlshead after bringing a cattle drive up from the Oklahoma territory and was surprised to find a military compound at one end of the town. No major line fort such as Kearny or Laramie but it did boast a blockhouse and a stockade. The second surprise was finding Molly Ludlum in Owlshead. It had been two years since he'd last seen her back in Kansas in a town called Cragsville. She'd worked for the local dance hall then, though she'd never been a fancy girl. But she'd always been a hellion, unbothered by how many eyebrows she raised, and he remembered all the pleasure times they'd had together. But small towns with pretensions could be cruel and he heard Molly had up and left one day, with a flare and a flounce, he was sure. In any case, she was gone when he'd stopped at Cragsville again and he'd never learned what had become of her.

Not until seven days ago when he'd ridden into Owlshead; Fargo smiled as he thought of how Molly had been as surprised and delighted as he. She'd flown into his arms in the middle of Main Street but quickly pulled away. "It's all different here, Skye," she had told him later. "I've a good job caring for Ed Kroger's two kids and I teach Sunday school every week."

"Sounds like you've changed into a right respectable young woman, Molly," he had commented. "You telling me you don't want to turn the clock back?"

Her smile had the sly mischievousness in it he used to know so well. "I'm not all that respectable I can't remember," she said. "I just have to be careful, now. No more sticking my tongue out at the world."

"I'll find the place, you find the time," he'd said, and her eyes had carried anticipation in their brown orbs. But though he'd found the little hollow, it had taken her a week to find the moment and now it had all exploded. Fargo grunted as his thoughts snapped off when he caught sight of honey-wheat hair. The girl was still riding hard along a ribbon of open land bordered by shadbush on one side and box elder on the other. But out of the corner of his eye he caught the movement in the shadbush and slowed the Ovaro immediately. He squinted into the distant trees and picked out the two horses moving swiftly after the girl, caught the flash of bronzed, naked torsos on agile Indian ponies.

He turned and sent the Ovaro into the box elder on the other side and put the horse into a gallop again. The girl was completely unaware of the two riders in the shadbush, he saw as she bent forward in the saddle, her eyes searching the open land ahead for signs of the calvary troop. The line of shadbush came to a sudden end another hundred yards on and Fargo had pulled almost abreast of the two riders when they burst into the open and pushed their ponies into a full-out gallop. He stayed in the box elder and saw the girl turn in the saddle, suddenly aware of her pursuers as they moved out on each side of her. She tried to coax more speed from her horse but the light brown mare was too tired to give any more. The two bronzed forms closed quickly on the girl and Fargo drew the Colt from its holster, grimaced, and dropped the gun back in place. Maybe there were others nearby. A shot would surely bring them on the run and he didn't want that.

He swore under his breath and took the Ovaro out of the box elder as the two Indians converged on the girl. He saw her try to swerve, strike out with her left arm as they came alongside her. But one reached from his horse, wrapped both arms around her waist, and pulled her from the saddle. He slowed his pony with his knees and half fell, half leaped to the ground with the girl still in his grip. The other Indian pulled to a halt, leaped to the ground, and grabbed the girl by the legs as she tried to kick herself free. Fargo's hand reached down to the narrow holster around his calf and he drew the double-edged throwing knife known in some places as an Arkansas toothpick. The first Indian had pinned the girl's arms behind her while the other began to pull at her skirt and Fargo caught a glimpse of long, smooth legs. They were both absorbed in their quarry and he was within a dozen yards of the pair when they became aware of him. The one pulling at the girl's skirt whirled, straightened, and yanked a tomahawk from the waist of his breechclout.

Fargo charged straight at him as he bent low in the saddle and threw the perfectly balanced blade underhanded. It whistled through the air and it took a second before the Indian saw it. He spun, tried to dive to his right, but the knife slammed into his side and buried itself to the hilt between his upper ribs. The man fell forward to his knees, the tomahawk dropping from his hand, and Fargo spurred the Ovaro straight at him. The man tried to get up and Fargo heard the horse's foreknee slam into his head as the Ovaro hurtled into and over him. Fargo reined up, turned, and leaped from the saddle to see the Indian on his back, his head a bloodied, smashed object and his side a stream of red.

The other brave threw the girl aside as he leaped to his feet and drew a jagged-edged elkbone knife from his waistband. He began to circle and Fargo saw the girl push to her feet, fear in her gray-blue eyes. "Get your horse," Fargo said to her as he began to circle with the Indian. "Get out of here and find those soldier boys." He flicked a glance at her and saw her hesitate. *"Now!"* he spit out, and she backed a pace, turned, and ran toward the light brown mare. His eyes were back on the brave and he saw the Indian decide not to try and stop her. The man had long arms and a thin body. He'd be quick of hand and foot, Fargo knew, and he drew the Colt from its holster, turned the gun in his hand to grip the barrel.

The Indian came forward as he circled, feinted with the bone knife, and Fargo refused to bite. He feinted again and once more Fargo didn't react. The next would not be a feint, Fargo knew, and he set himself as the Indian came in again. The red man's arm came up, made a half feint and then hurtled forward with the bone knife in a flat, slashing blow. Fargo drew his stomach in as he leaped backward with both feet and the knife grazed the front of his shirt. He brought the butt of the gun up in a short arc but the Indian's quickness pulled him away and the blow missed. Fargo ducked away to avoid a second follow-through but the Indian was careful as well as quick and set himself again before moving forward.

The flash of wheat-honey hair racing away caught Fargo's eye as he circled with the Indian and this time he tried a feint. The brave ducked away and Fargo swung the butt of the gun again and once more the man pulled away. But this time the brave swung his body into a crouch, coming forward with quick, alternating steps, both hands moving spasmodically. Fargo gave ground and the brave followed until, with a lightning-quick motion, the Indian threw a chopping left fist and as Fargo ducked away from the blow, lunged with the bone knife. Fargo let himself go down on his knees as the weapon grazed his temple and he silently cursed the man's surefootedness. He managed to bring his own left up in a short arc, all the strength of his shoulder muscles behind the blow, and sank his fist into the Indian's belly. The man grunted in pain as he staggered back, and with a few inches more room, Fargo brought the gun butt around in an upward arc.

The brave twisted away but the blow caught him a glancing blow alongside the cheek and he fell to one side. Fargo charged after him, the Colt raised to smash down on his foe's head. But he'd been too eager and it was too late when he saw the kick flung backward at him. The blow caught him in the stomach and he went backward in pain, his feet going out from under him. He saw the long-armed body charging, the bone knife thrust out as if it were a lance. On his back, he rolled and the knife buried itself in the ground a fraction of an inch from his ear. He tried to roll again and felt one long, sinewy arm wrap itself around his neck. "Goddamn," Fargo swore as he used his powerful shoulders to push himself to his knees. The brave clung to him, one arm tight around Fargo's neck, a grip that would have forced most men back choking for breath. But he was too light to hold Fargo's powerful body and the big man rose, the Indian still clinging to him almost as a child clings piggy-back to its father.

Fargo bent forward, swung his body in a tight circle, and sent the brave sailing from him. He whirled as the Indian hit the ground, charged at the thin form, and

16

saw the Indian scramble to his feet, managing to avoid the first sweeping blow of the heavy Colt. The brave continued to scramble to get away; and in frustration and fury, Fargo brought the butt of the gun down with all his strength on the Indian's calf. The man gave a gasp of pain as his leg collapsed under him and he fell forward, tried to scramble again, but his numbed calf refused to respond. He whirled, tried a kick with his other leg, and Fargo took the blow against the side of his thigh as he brought the Colt down in a whistling arc. The heavy gun butt smashed into the man's temple and Fargo heard the sound of bone splintering. He drew back as the Indian twitched, his long arms flailing against his sides spasmodically. Then he lay still.

Fargo pushed himself to his feet, turned the Colt in his hand, and swept the surrounding terrain with a long, probing glance. He saw nothing move, no other bronzed horsemen appear, and he walked to the first lifeless form, retrieved his throwing knife, and wiped it clean on the grass. He returned the knife to its calf holster and pulled himself onto the Ovaro and sent the horse northward. He'd just crested a low hill when he saw the cavalry platoon riding toward him at a fast canter and he saw the honey-wheat hair glistening in the sunlight alongside the officer at the head of the column.

He halted, waited, and counted sixteen troopers as the platoon reached him. "First Lieutenant Baker," the young officer said as he waved the troop to a halt. Fargo took in a face that hadn't been shaving for too many years, an even-featured serious face that tried to make earnestness hide its youth.

"Don't stop on my account," Fargo said blandly. "Go on and see to those wagons."

"Move out," the lieutenant called to his platoon and

Fargo saw the girl stay in place as the troopers swept past, her gray-blue eyes searching his face.

"I was afraid we'd find you'd been killed," she said.

"I don't kill easily," Fargo remarked.

"Are you coming along?"

"Why not?"

"But you don't think there's any point in hurrying," the girl said.

"Go to the head of the class," Fargo replied.

She frowned. "Why bother coming along?"

"Curiosity," he said, and saw her lips tighten.

"We'll talk later," she said, and sent the light brown mare into a fast canter after the platoon.

Fargo followed at a leisurely trot. He was in no hurry to see what he was certain they'd find and what he had seen all too often. He slowed as he rode past the lifeless forms of the two Indians who had attacked the girl, paused to look at the beadwork on their moccasins and the design on the armband one wore. He nodded to himself, his mouth a grim line as he went on.

Fargo nostrils drew in the acrid odor of the burnt wood

2

Fargo's nostrils drew in the acrid odor of burnt wood
before he reached the top of the land where it dipped
into a saucerlike valley. The others were there, he saw
when he edged down the slope, grouped around the
remains of two charred wagons. Small clouds of smoke
drifted upward and hung in the air over the two wagons, not unlike a dark and mordant halo. He saw the
honey-wheat hair off to one side as the lieutenant had
his troopers picking up what few personal possessions
lay scattered on the ground.

Fargo rode up to the girl and dismounted, letting his
glance slowly travel across the scene. He felt the frown
touch his brow. "You were right," the girl said. "It
was all over before we got here."

"Being right doesn't always make you feel good,"
Fargo said, and dismounted. He felt the girl's eyes on
him as he bent down and picked up an arrow. He
studied the bands of vegetable-dye color markings near
the quills. "Arapaho," he grunted. "So were the other
two that chased you."

The girl nodded and her gray-blue eyes studied him.
"What's your name, big man?"

"Fargo, Skye Fargo. Some call me the Trailsman."

"I'm Bess," she said in answer to the question in his lake-blue eyes.

"That's all?" he grunted.

"For now," she said.

"Savages. Damn savages," the voice cut in, and they turned to see the young officer coming toward them.

"Anything else?" Fargo asked, and drew a frown.

"What else is there? Seems to me that's more than enough," Lieutenant Baker said.

"Nothing strike you as funny about this attack?" Fargo asked mildly.

The lieutenant scanned the wagons again, frowning as he returned his gaze to the big man at his elbow. "Such as?" he queried.

"No one left," Fargo said. "Not one man with his head bashed in by a tomahawk. Not one body skewered to a wagon by arrows. Not one woman left raped and slit from ear to ear."

"I assume because they decided to take prisoners," the lieutenant said. "I've heard Indians sometimes take prisoners to keep as slaves or sell off to other tribes."

"You said the key word, sonny," Fargo grunted. "*Sometimes*, and never like this."

"You apparently know a lot about Indians, Fargo," the girl said.

"I've learned, more than I ever wanted to know," Fargo said with grimness in his voice.

"What do you think this means?" she asked.

Fargo shrugged. "Wouldn't know, but it's damn strange."

"I must go along with the logical assumption that they needed slaves," the lieutenant said.

"You do that," Fargo commented, and fastened his

eyes on the girl. It was the first moment he'd had to really take her in, and he saw she had thin blond eyebrows to match the honey-wheat hair, nice red lips, full when they weren't tight with disapproval. He saw square shoulders and longish breasts that curved into fullness under her shirt, a narrow waist and a long torso. Tall, he observed, and lean and willowy with an attractiveness despite the cool control she kept in her face.

"You'll come back to the compound with us, Fargo," the lieutenant said. "The major will want a statement from everyone, the young lady and yourself."

"I'll be along later," Fargo said, and started to climb onto the Ovaro.

"This is important, Fargo. I must insist you ride in with us now," the young officer said.

"Don't insist, sonny," Fargo said calmly from the saddle. "I'll stop by later."

"Mr. Fargo has his own ideas of what's important, Lieutenant," the girl said, and Fargo heard the taunting reproof in her tone. "With you, Lieutenant, it's duty before pleasure. With Mr. Fargo, it's pleasure before duty."

Fargo turned a slow smile at her. "Couldn't have said it better myself, honey," he remarked, and walked the Ovaro back up the slope.

"Ask for Major Devereaux at the compound," the lieutenant called after him. Fargo waved a hand back and continued up the slope and heard the platoon ride on behind him. At the top of the slope, he paused, saw the column vanish in the other direction, and he slowly made a wide circle around the dip of land. He continued to ride slowly as his eyes searched the ground and he reined to a halt a dozen yards away, leaned from the saddle, and read the hoofprints in the soft soil. The Arapaho had split up into small parties, he

21

saw, at least three of them. Two had pulled a pack of extra horses behind them, he observed as he studied the tracks. Every part of the attack had been carefully planned, Fargo noted grimly, and he turned the Ovaro around, set the horse into a trot, and rode back the way he had come.

In the distance, Shadow Mountain rose into the blue sky as if it were a reminder of how many others had come to fight and die for this land. The Indians had been here first, but then the Spaniards had come to call it the red land and give it the name *Colorado*. The French explorers and trappers were next and then the American with his wagons and settlements. Sometimes, the Cheyenne forayed from Wyoming to the north and the Pawnee and Utes raided when they felt bold; but the Arapaho claimed this land as theirs, against all others, white or red. Still, Fargo frowned in thought, the attack on the wagon train stabbed at him. It stank of its own rottenness, something more than usual savage fury.

He pushed the frown from his brow as he came into sight of the cedar grove and slowed when he neared the hollow. He nosed the pinto through the trees and came to a halt at the edge of the hollow to watch Molly step out from behind a cluster of shrubs. He slid from the saddle and she wrapped her arms around him at once. "I kept being afraid something would go wrong. Did you find her?" she asked.

"Yes, and the platoon," Fargo answered. "Followed them to the wagons."

"I don't want to hear the rest," Molly said. "Not now. You're back and I want the rest of the day as we'd planned."

"Best idea I've heard so far," Fargo said, swept her into his arms, and set her down on the soft star moss. He began to shed his clothes as Molly pulled her blouse off and once again he enjoyed her quiet loveliness. His lips closed around one modest breast, pulled gently, and felt the brown-pink nipple immediately grow firm. Molly's hands dug into his back as she gasped out small cooing sounds and he felt her stir under his touch. Her slightly rounded belly lifted, quivered as his hands moved gently over the smooth skin, moved down further, pressed into the fibrous, curly patch, and moved down still further.

"Oh, oh, God," Molly breathed as his fingers touched the luscious warmth, gently spread the fleshy lips, and she quivered harder, her thighs falling open. "Oh, Fargo, too long . . . oh, too long. Come to me, Jeez, come to me," Molly murmured, and her knees rose, moving apart, the eternal invitation of the body consumed with desire. Her hand reached along his hip, down his leg, and almost darted across his flat abdomen to curl around his pulsating firmness. "Ah, aaaah . . ." Molly groaned and turned her hips, pushing her damp triangle at him. "Please, Fargo, now, now . . ." she entreated, and her voice trailed away in a breathy gasp.

He moved atop her and her legs clasped around him, pressing tight, and he slid slowly into her and she screamed with delight. "Oh, my God, oh, oh, yes, yes . . . oh yes," Molly murmured, and pushed her pelvis upward to take in all of him, drew back as he did, and rammed herself forward with an explosion of wanting. "Please, please, oh God, Fargo," she cried against his face, pushing harder and harder against him, and he felt the tightness gather inside her, tiny contractions that grew stronger, faster, until they became a seemingly endless chain of warm, wet clutchings, and suddenly she arched her neck backward and all the yesterdays flooded over him. He rammed hard into her, as deep as he could, and pressed against the soft wall. Molly's scream of utter pleasure spiraled around the little hollow as though it had a life of its own. "Now, now, oh, now," Molly gasped. "Uuunueeeeeiiiiii . . . oh, yes, now." He let himself explode with her and she screamed again as she clung to him, lifting herself almost completely off the ground against him, her body pressed so hard against him it seemed as though she were trying to imprint flesh on flesh, weld touch and feel together in one never-ending tapestry of ecstasy.

But finally, still quivering, she fell back and her legs and arms grew limp around him, opened and fell away and he heard her soft cry of protest. "Over, damn . . . it always ends . . . not fair," she murmured, and turned to him, buried her face into his chest. He stroked her gently and she lay still in his arms. Finally he heard her whispered words. "Careful, you'll start things up again," she said. "A starved person isn't satisfied with one meal."

His hands moved slowly down her back, came to rest against the small, firm rear. "Nothing wrong with a second meal," he murmured, and she turned, offered her modest breasts upward.

"No, nothing at all," she breathed, and brought his face down to the lovely mounds. Again, he took first one, then the other in his lips, and Molly's arms closed around him at once. This time she took longer to explode in ecstasy with him but her scream again circled the little hollow in sheer joy. "God, this turning the clock back is more wonderful than I imagined," she said later as she lay beside him.

"You could work on finding another time," Fargo said.

"Yes, but I'll still have to be careful," Molly said.

"I won't be staying on for too long," he reminded her.

"You never do," she said with a touch of rue in her voice. "I'll work on it."

"Who is this Ed Kroger you work for?" Fargo asked.

"He owns the general store and he's sort of the unofficial mayor. Emily Kroger runs the store with him. That's why I take care of their kids," Molly said, and sat up as the late afternoon shadows began to reach into the hollow. "Time to start back," she sighed, reaching for her blouse. He cupped his hand under one modest breast before it disappeared under the garment. Molly gave a little sigh of pleasure and held his hand there until she shook him away finally. "I wish you'd come visit regularly," she said. "But I know better than to expect that."

"Maybe I can." Fargo laughed. "You never know where I'll show up." He rose, pulled clothes on, and strapped on his gunbelt as Molly finished tucking her blouse in neatly. "I have to pay a visit to the army compound when I get to town," he told her.

Molly cast a glance at him that held sudden apprehension in it. "Those two wagons, God, I hope they weren't ours," she said. "They'd be heading back about this time."

"Ours?" he echoed.

"Every year a committee from town, mostly women but with a few men, journeys to Grand Junction. They spend a week there picking up all kinds of special things for the harvest festival," Molly explained.

"Harvest is months away," Fargo said.

"Yes, but they bring back things the townswomen spend all summer making and preparing for the festival, fancy material, special spices we never get here, fancy goods and fancy foods packed in mason jars. Folks from nearby towns all come to the Owlshead harvest festival and we make money for the town

25

treasury. It helps prepare everyone for the long winter months when it's hard to get together."

"The troopers took back whatever personal possessions were left scattered around. Maybe they'll give the answer when they're examined," Fargo said.

"Yes, they should," Molly said, and sent her horse into a canter. Owlshead came into sight soon enough and she halted, leaned from the saddle to press her lips to his. "I'll work on finding another time for us. Don't ride out without saying good-bye," she told him.

"Wouldn't think of it." He laughed, slapped her on the leg, and let her ride on ahead of him into town. He followed slowly and the lavender light of early dusk had begun to sift down when he rode into Owlshead. He moved down along the main street and noticed the usual bustle and activity seemed to be missing as only a half-dozen wagons and one buckboard lined the street. He rode on into the army compound that made up the north end of town, dismounted, and took in the long troop barracks at one side of the compound and at least a half-dozen smaller cabins that lined the opposite side. Two sentries manned the top of the stockade walls with indolent casualness but at the far corner of the compound he saw several troopers on guard outside what was clearly the stockade jailhouse.

He walked toward the separate building where the company flag flew from the roof and a corporal outside brought his carbine up to attention at once. "Yes, sir?" the soldier asked.

"I'm here to see Major Devereaux," Fargo said. "Lieutenant Baker told me to stop by."

The corporal disappeared into the building to return moments later. "Please wait here," he said as he ushered Fargo into an outer office with several hard-backed chairs and two arched doorways, one with the door closed, the other hung with burlap drapes. He started to ease down onto one of the chairs when he heard the burlap rustle and rose as he saw the flash of honey-wheat hair push through the drapes. The girl came out and met his gaze with her gray-blue eyes scanning the chiseled handsomeness of his face.

"Didn't expect to see you still here," Fargo said. "You been waiting to ask me how I enjoyed my afternoon?"

The gray-blue eyes narrowed. "Hardly," she snapped disdainfully. "But I did wait to talk to you alone. I'm Major Devereaux's daughter."

Fargo felt his brows lift. "How come Lieutenant Baker didn't seem to know that?" he asked.

"The lieutenant was on field duty when I arrived. I've only been here for three days," she said, starting to add more when the door opened and a man stepped into the room. Fargo took in a trim, lean figure in a crisp, pressed uniform, graying hair with still a trace of sandiness in it, a handsome man with the girl's even features but none of the strength in her face. Where her eyes were bold, his were shaded with caution; where her mouth held firmness, his had little lines of weakness at the corners.

"I've been waiting for you, Mr. Fargo. Lieutenant Baker seemed uncertain as to whether you'd appear," the major said with a hint of sardonic humor.

"He's young," Fargo said, and the major smiled at the unsaid in the reply.

"Please come in," Major Devereaux said, and led the way into an office where a desk, chairs, and an old file cabinet all but filled in the room. "You're the one they call the Trailsman," he said. "You have a reputation that carries. Sam Donald of the Seventh has spoke of you."

27

Fargo nodded. "Yes, I've worked with Sam."

"My daughter told me you were very helpful to her this afternoon," the major said, and Fargo's eyes sought out Bess Devereaux.

"Helpful?" He frowned and saw that she had the decency to look uncomfortable.

"I told father how you'd directed me to the platoon," Bess Devereaux said, and her gray-blue eyes carried a plea for silence.

He thought for a moment, let his lips purse, and watched the plea deepen in her eyes. Finally he decided to let curiosity hold back the acid reply that had come to his lips. "Glad I could help," he said, and saw the flash of gratefulness touch Bess Devereaux's eyes.

"Those two wagons were filled with the wives, husbands, sons, and daughters of Owlshead families," the major said.

"They were the special-committee wagons?" Fargo said, and the major nodded. Damn, Fargo bit out silently. Molly's fears had come home to roost.

"That makes this especially distressing," the major said, but sounded more annoyed than grieved. "Just more of the same unbridled Indian savagery."

Fargo heard Bess Devereaux's voice cut in, cool curiosity in the tone of it. "Fargo doesn't think this attack is more of the same," she commented.

Her father's half smile held irritating tolerance, Fargo saw. "Yes, the lieutenant told me you thought the attack had something strange about it," the major said to him. "But I'm afraid I must go along with Lieutenant Baker. The Indians needed prisoners as slaves."

"Only a few of the tribes, and never this way," Fargo said.

"How do you mean that?" the major questioned, the hint of sardonic humor staying in his face.

"The Crow take slaves. So do the Sioux and the

Comanche. Apache and Kiowa too. But most tribes don't take prisoners except to use as sacrifice. Those that do almost always take young girls and women, sometimes very young boys. They consider grown men too much trouble. The Arapaho don't much go in for using slaves and this time they took everybody on those wagons. That doesn't fit."

"Come, now, Fargo. The Indian is hardly consistent in his behavior," the major said condescendingly.

"Neither is the cougar, to those who don't know him. Those who take the time to understand the cougar know that he's very consistent in his behavior," Fargo replied evenly.

The major offered another smile of irritating tolerance. "We all tend to rationalize, Fargo," he said, and Fargo returned a slow smile. Major Devereaux, he decided, let an air of tolerant superiority cloak his lack of field knowledge. Or perhaps he was just too full of conceit. Either way, the man wasn't his kind of post commander. "I'll send a squad out come morning. We'll track them down," the major said.

"Good luck," Fargo remarked.

The major's smile widened. "Do I detect a lack of confidence?" he asked.

"Bull's-eye." Fargo smiled back. "Nice meeting you." He turned and strolled from the office, ignoring Bess Devereaux. Outside, he found the night had settled down and he started to lead the Ovaro through the compound when he heard the hurried footsteps coming up behind him. He paused, turned, and saw the honey-wheat hair, bright even in the darkness. She halted beside him and her longish breasts lifted as she drew a deep breath, the rounded fullness at the bottom pressing into her blouse to pull the fabric taut.

"Go on, ask," she said. "I owe you an explanation, among other things."

29

Fargo felt the irritation inside himself surge up. "What was all that being helpful shit?" he snapped out. "Why didn't you tell Daddy I saved your ass, in more ways than one?"

He saw her lips tighten as she gathered another deep breath. "He was furious when he learned I'd gone out riding alone. Only telling him that I'd done something good made him calm down. If I told him what really almost happened to me, he'd have me on the way back to Missouri already," she said.

"Maybe that'd be best."

"No, not now. I turned twenty-one a month ago and decided to do what I always wanted to do, get to know my father. He and my mother separated years ago and I've only seen him for short visits. I've always had to admire him from afar, you might say. Now I'll do it close up," Bess Devereaux explained. "I didn't want anything to get in the way of that so I bent the truth some."

"You did," Fargo said, and felt his reactions to her father skip through his mind. It wasn't just a matter of unfavorable first impressions, though he usually trusted his gut feelings. It was also knowing the army. They kept their top officers for the big line forts and important field commands. Out-of-the-way places such as Owlshead got the tired and the incompetent, the weak links and the misfits. It was one way the army handled its personnel problems. It didn't always work that way, he admitted silently to himself. But often enough.

"What are you thinking?" Bess Devereaux asked, interrupting his thoughts.

"I'm hoping you find everything the way you want to find it," Fargo said.

"Thank you. I'm sure I will," she said, and paused, her eyes studying him. "You're a strange man, Fargo," she said.

"Meaning what?" he queried.

"You wouldn't stop indulging yourself to go help the wagons, yet you risked your life to save me," the young woman said.

"I don't waste time playing with loaded dice," Fargo said, and saw her frown back. "The wagons were past helping. You weren't," he added.

She gave a wry little snort. "No matter, I am in your debt, more than I can repay," she said. "And I am grateful to you."

He nodded. "Stay out of trouble," he said, and walked on with the Ovaro following.

He paused as he heard her call out after him. "Why the woods?" she asked, a hint of teasing in her voice.

"You're awful curious."

"You take note of something unusual. So do I," she returned. "Do I get an answer?"

"There were reasons. Everything has reasons," he said, and continued on. Female curiosity, he smiled to himself, worse than a kitten's. The compound gates were wide open and he passed through, nodded to a lone soldier standing nearby. He strolled along the main street of town and saw small knots of figures talking in subdued tones. The only bright light and sound came from inside the saloon and dance hall in the center of town. He tethered the horse to the hitching post and stepped beneath the sign that read:

DOLLY'S
DRINKS, DAMES, AND DANCING

Pushing through the double doors, he went inside, and though the bar was fairly crowded, he saw as many girls as customers at the tables that circled the small dance floor. A small man in a green shirt and eyeshade pounded a tinkly piano with more accuracy than enthusiasm.

Fargo saw the woman come toward him, powder and paint and a blond wig, all of it trying hard to hide the years, maybe fifty of them, he guessed, and all failing. But her smile was warm and without the mechanical twist so many dance hall madams had as stock in trade. "Welcome, big man," she said. "What'll it be?"

"Bourbon," Fargo said, and Dolly signaled to the bartender.

"Sit down," the woman said, gestured to a table. "Plenty of room tonight, all because of that dammed attack on the wagons."

"Didn't expect it'd bother you this much. You don't exactly get a family trade, I wouldn't think," Fargo commented as he eased into a chair beside the table.

"A lot of my customers know folks who were in those wagons. Some work for them or their friends. I guess they figure it'd be disrespectful to go drinking and dancing. I can understand that," Dolly said, and lowered an ample figure in a flounced silk gown into the next chair. She'd let the years harden the outside more than the inside, Fargo decided. "You're new in town," the woman said, sizing him up with a long, appreciative glance.

"Don't figure to stay long," Fargo said. He took the bourbon from the bartender as the man brought it to the table, drew in a long sip of the amber liquid. "Good bourbon, Dolly," he commented.

"Don't serve any rotgut here," Dolly said. The sudden shout from a nearby table interrupted anything she was going to add. "Another drink," the voice said, both words thick and slurred. Fargo looked across at the man and saw the watery eyes of the perpetual drunk, graying, unkempt hair atop a long, thin face that seemed made of lines. Beneath it, a thin body and spindly arms tried to sit up straight and swayed back and forth. If a sapling could be old, it would look like that, Fargo found himself thinking despite the incongruity of the thought.

"One more, Titus," Dolly said, and gestured to the bartender.

"One more," the man echoed. "Got to drink one more to stupid-ass Major Devereaux. Goddamn fool." A girl brought the shot glass of whiskey to the table and Fargo watched the thin arm lift the glass to the weathered, lined face. He watched the man down the whiskey in one, quick gulp and exhale a long, wheezing breath. The watery blue eyes tried to focus on Dolly. "Told him, I did. Told the stupid-ass fool," the man said, barely managing to form the words. "Told him," he breathed, coughed, and his head fell forward onto the table.

Dolly motioned to the bartender. "Get Charley to help you take him home," she said.

"You know what he was talking about?" Fargo asked the woman.

"No," she said.

"He's one of your regulars, I take it," Fargo said.

Dolly cast a level glance at him. "A man pays, he's got the right to drink," she said. "Besides, Titus has earned the right."

"How's that?" Fargo queried.

"Titus saw more people through the Colorado territory alive than any man," the woman said. "For years, he was the best damn guide in this part of the country."

Fargo felt the frown dig into his brow. "Titus . . ." he mused aloud. "Would that be Titus Toomey?" he asked, and Dolly nodded. "I'll be damned. I used to hear about him. He used to scout for the Fifth Cavalry out of Wyoming too."

"That's him," Dolly said.

"What happened?" Fargo asked.

The woman shrugged. "Never heard. All I know is that now he does odd jobs, some for me, enough to earn him bottle money."

"Too bad," Fargo said, and watched the bartender and another man half drag and half carry Titus Toomey out a side entrance of the dance hall. He finished his bourbon when the woman went to tend bar and walked outside into the night. He continued to walk along the street, holding the Ovaro by the reins, and he had just reached the general store when he saw the figure step out from the side of the two-story frame structure and hurry toward him, a nightrobe clutched to her.

"I waited and hoped you'd come this way," Molly said.

"You ready to turn back the clock again?" Fargo asked, surprise and instant anticipation pulling at him.

"No, you said you were going to stop at the compound. What did you find out?" Molly said. "Emily Kroger was in those wagons."

Fargo grimaced in sympathy. "Didn't find out much except that the major's sending a squad out come morning," he answered. She caught something in his tone and peered hard at him.

"You don't figure they'll find anyone," Molly said.

"They could get lucky," he told her.

"What else is bothering you?" she asked. He smiled inwardly. She'd always been quick to pick up on little things.

"I'm not sure," he said. "But something's not right."

"You can help the major, Fargo. You're the Trailsman. Nobody can track the way you can."

"Major Devereaux's not a man who admits he needs help."

"Then look for them on your own."

34

"Maybe." He shrugged and she came to lean against him.

"Promise me you'll do what you can," she murmured.

"I'll try," he said, and she clung for an other moment before stepping back, her small face grave. She turned and hurried to the house and he waited till he heard the door latch close before he swung onto the pinto. He rode out of Owlshead, across a gentle slope, and halted at the crest. The night was dark, a new moon little more than a sliver in the sky. But there was something more than the darkness. He felt the gnawing premonition of trouble. It hung in the night dark, an unseen presence but as real as the horse under him.

He turned the pinto, rode into a stand of cottonwoods, found a spot to bed down, and stretched out on his bedroll. He lay still and the words of an old drunk suddenly swam through his mind. *Told him, I did. Told him.* Just the rantings of a liquor-sodden imagination? Or something more, Fargo mused as he closed his eyes and drew sleep around himself.

3

Bright sun probed through the leaves to wake him and he found a stream nearby where he washed and dressed. A thick stand of upland cranberry, the fruit the Indians called *kinnikinic*, afforded a sweet-tart breakfast and he let his eyes scan the terrain. The major would have his squad out and riding hard by now, Fargo surmised. They'd go to where the attack took place and try to pick up a trail from there. He let a wry sound escape his lips. They'd find only trails that led nowhere. They'd have to scour the land on their own and they'd be too noisy and too visible.

Fargo turned the Ovaro west, rode down the slope and into a long valley thick with staghorn sumac. His gaze swept the land as he rode, seeing where others only looked, reading the wild signs as most men read books. Deer had crossed only minutes before, he saw, in flight, taking long bounds that dug their sharp hooves deep into the ground, and he slowed at once. Something had made them flee and he found the answer a few yards on where he saw the marks of four Indian ponies. He turned the pinto to follow the trail that led through the sumac and the land dipped lower, the brush beginning to thin out. He frowned as he saw the ponies had suddenly gone into a gallop and he spurred the pinto on when he heard the scream, a woman's voice filled with pain and terror.

He sent the Ovaro racing forward and the farmhouse came into sight, a small corral fence at the back. He cursed at the scene he took in with a sweeping glance. Two Arapaho dragged a woman across the ground, one holding her by the hair, one by the arms. At the far corner of the house, two more braves flung a boy over a broad-backed Indian pony. Fargo drew the Colt as he saw the Indian holding the woman by the hair raise a long-bladed knife. He took quick aim and fired just as the Arapaho started to bring the blade down in a swooping arc. The shot caught the man full in the chest and he flew backward as he erupted in a shower of blood and bone.

The other brave whirled and flung his tomahawk at the horseman that raced at him. Fargo glimpsed the short-handled ax as it hurtled at him in a deadly-straight line. He had time only to drop from the saddle and he heard the tomahawk whistle past him as he hit the ground. He managed to twist, land on one shoulder, roll, and complete a somersault that brought him up on one knee in time to see the Indian lunging at him with a bone knife in one hand. Fargo fired the Colt from his hips and the attacker screamed in agony, clutched at his groin as his breechclout suddenly turned red. He stumbled, dripping blood down his legs, fell forward facedown to lie in the still grotesqueness of the dead.

Fargo whirled and saw the other two Arapaho almost out of sight as they raced off with the boy. "Oh, God, my boy, my boy," he heard the woman cry out. "They've taken Jimmy." He rose, saw her on her hands and knees, and he pulled her to her feet. "He's only fourteen, dear God," she gasped as she stared into the distant trees. Fargo frowned into the distance with her. The other two braves hadn't even tried to help their brothers. They had only one thing in mind, to make off with the boy.

He was still frowning when he turned to the woman. "You've a husband somewhere?" he asked.

"In town, buying feed," she said, "I'm Irma Fulton."

"Come on, I'll get you to town. You have a wagon here?" Fargo asked.

"Tom took it with him but I can ride our old mare," Irma Fulton said, and stared into the trees again. "My Jimmy, they just up and took him. Oh, dear God."

"Get the horse," Fargo said, and the woman hurried to a half-faced shed behind the house to return leading a mottled brown mare.

"Those savages came from west of here. Ned and Betty Ryan live only a mile that way. We ought to see if they're all right," the woman said.

"Good enough. You lead the way," Fargo agreed, and climbed onto the Ovaro. He rode a half-dozen strides behind Irma Fulton, his gaze sweeping the land, one hand on the Colt at his hip. When they reached the Ryan place, he sent the Ovaro past the woman and arrived at the house first to see the man on the ground, by the open doorway, an ugly red bruise on his temple. Fargo leaped from the horse, knelt down beside the figure, and saw that the man was alive, the bruise on his temple the only mark on him. Gray-haired, pushing fifty or more, Ryan groaned as Fargo lifted him up against the doorjamb. His eyelids fluttered and came open and he stared, took a moment to focus. He blinked finally, and the horror came into his face instantly.

"Betty, my God, Betty," the man said. Fargo helped pull him to his feet and he saw Irma Fulton. "Irma,

they took Betty," he said. "I never heard them coming and suddenly there they were."

"How many?" Fargo asked.

"Three. One hit me with the back of his tomahawk
while the other two grabbed Betty."

"Four of them struck our place. They took Jimmy,"
Irma Fulton said. "God knows what would've happened to me if this man hadn't come by." She stopped
and her eyes went to Fargo, grew wide with apology.
"Dear God, I never did ask your name, mister. I'm
sorry," she said.

"Fargo, Skye Fargo," the Trailsman said. "Get your
horse, Ryan. You'd best come into town with us."
The man nodded and hurried off to return on a gray
gelding. Fargo mounted up and rode ahead slowly
enough for the two shaken people to stay close on his
heels, and he let thoughts tumble through his mind.
Two small raiding parties, he frowned, obviously out
to take a captive in each attack and leave someone
behind. He grimaced. The two raids didn't fit the
usual pattern, any more than the attack on the wagons
fit. He hadn't information enough for the game of
speculation and turned off his thoughts to concentrate
on getting to Owlshead.

When they rode into town, Irma Fulton spotted her
husband and rushed up to him, and Fargo rode on to
the compound with Ned Ryan. He dismounted and it
was Bess Devereaux who opened the office door for
him, a dark green blouse setting off the blazing soft
beauty of her honey-wheat hair Her eyes moved past
him to Ned Ryan and she saw the red welt on his
temple. She ushered them both into her father's office
at once, leaned against a chair as she listened to Fargo
tell of the two attacks. When he finished, Fargo saw
the lines of tenseness that had come into her lovely,
even-featured face.

"You poor man," Major Devereaux said to Ryan with just the right note of sympathy tempered by firm authority, Fargo noted. "My squad won't be back till late afternoon but they may well cross paths with those raiding parties and bring Mrs. Ryan back. The Fulton boy too," the major said. Fargo felt Bess Devereaux's eyes on him as he let a grim wryness touch his face. "Meanwhile, it might be best for you and the Fultons to stay the night here at the compound or in town somewhere," the major went on to Ryan. "I'll send a detail to talk to the Fultons and help you both fetch your things."

"Appreciate that, Major," Ryan said, and Major Devereaux walked from the office with him. Fargo heard him giving orders to the corporal outside as he turned to meet Bess Devereaux's eyes as she continued to study him.

"You think Father's taking this too much in stride, don't you?" she asked.

"Can't say," he answered.

"Don't patronize me, Fargo" the girl snapped. "You don't think his troopers will cross paths with those raiding parties, do you?"

"Not unless the Arapaho all suddenly go deaf, dumb, and blind," Fargo returned.

"What'll you say if they come back with Ned Ryan's wife and the Fulton boy?" Bess asked almost tauntingly.

"Amen," Fargo replied.

"Damn, you are a hard-nosed man," she said.

"Lucky for you," he said, and her lips tightened.

"Yes, I haven't forgotten that," she murmured. "I just don't think you've enough respect for Father's opinions."

Fargo took in her loveliness, his eyes moving over the honey-wheat hair and the eyebrows to match, the longish breasts that curved into beautiful fullness. "Why don't you get out of here while you still can? Go back home for now," he said.

"You think I can't take what I might see?"

"No, what you might find out."

The gray-blue eyes flared. "That's a rotten thing to say."

"Maybe," he grunted.

"You know, some people can't take being disagreed with. I'm wondering if you're one of them," she said.

"Keep wondering, honey," he said, and started from the office as the major returned.

"It seems you do have a talent for showing up in the nick of time, Fargo," the major said with a condescending smile edging his lips. "That could be dangerous."

"It has been, mostly for others," Fargo said.

"You convinced these raids are just the usual random savagery, now?" Major Devereaux asked.

"Nope," Fargo said.

"You're a stubborn man." The major smiled.

"So I've been told," Fargo said, and strode from the office. Outside, he led the Ovaro down the street to the dance hall, dropped the reins over the hitching post, and pushed his way through the doors. The place was empty except for an old man sweeping the floor and the bartender and Dolly cleaning up the bar area. He took a moment to recognize the woman without her wig and decided she looked a lot less brittle.

"Didn't figure you for an early drinker, big man," Dolly said with some surprise.

"I'm looking to talk to Titus Toomey," Fargo said.

"*Hah!* Now, that may take some doing, friend," the woman answered.

Fargo frowned. "Meaning what exactly?"

"Titus was waiting when I came downstairs. He

took two bottles. Knowing Titus, I'd say he was pretty near finished with both by now," Dolly said.

Fargo glanced at the bartender. "You took him home last night. Where's that?"

"The abandoned grain shed at the south end of town," the man answered.

"I want the biggest damn kettle of black coffee you can make," Fargo said to Dolly, and flung a handful of coins on the bar.

"That'll get you a heap of coffee," Dolly said. "Give me a few minutes." She hurried into the back of the saloon and he sat down at one of the tables and waited till she reappeared carrying a deep, iron pot of steaming, black coffee. "Tin cup's in the kettle," she said.

"Obliged." Fargo nodded and strode from the saloon with the kettle in hand. He led the Ovaro through the town and finally spotted the broken planking of what had once been a silo a few dozen yards beyond the edge of the town. Beside it, a flat-roofed, sagging shed still bore the word *GRANARY* on it and somehow remained upright though it leaned to one side. He halted and heard the offpitch, reedy voice singing from inside the shed. His eyes swept the one side of the shed and spotted an old water trough almost full with rainwater. He nodded in satisfaction and eased himself through the partially open door and the singing grew louder and took on slurred form.

> "My horses ain't hungry,
>   they won't eat your hay,
> Sit here beside me
>   as long as you stay,
> My wagon is loaded and rollin' away. . . ."

Fargo managed to recognize the wavering tune and the words that somehow came through and he followed the voice to where he saw the tin, spindly-armed figure in trousers and undershirt. Titus Toomey leaned his head back against the wall of the shed as he sang, an almost empty bottle in one hand. The abandoned shed, Fargo saw, was littered with broken packing crates, barrels, empty bottles, and cobwebs. A torn mattress lay in one corner and the place smelled of stale whiskey and vomit. Titus Toomey was perhaps too far down the road to change, Fargo grunted, but the man had said something that needed explaining, words that had been either the meaningless mouthings of an old drunk or words that held a terrible truth cloaked in liquor.

He had to find out, Fargo muttered to himself as he stepped forward and, with one long-armed sweep of his hand, knocked the whiskey bottle from Titus Toomey's grasp. He stood over the man and watched Titus Toomey take a long moment to put together what had happened. Finally the frown came over the lined, weathered face and the man stared up at him. "What's the damn idea?" he demanded.

"Want to talk to you," Fargo said.

"Go to hell. No talk. Get me another bottle, damn you," Titus Toomey slurred, and started to push himself up, sliding his back against the wall. Fargo let him draw himself up straight. "You owe me a bottle," the man flung out.

Fargo set the kettle of coffee down. "No more bottles. We're going to talk," he said.

"Talk? I'll show you talk," the thin form spat out. One thin arm came up in a roundhouse swing. Fargo didn't move as the blow went harmlessly past his face. Reluctantly, he brought a short left up and, holding the force back, sank it into the man's stomach. "Aaagh, Jesus," Titus gasped, falling forward on his hands and knees. "Agh, agh, Jesus," he said as he proceeded to throw up.

Fargo waited till the thin form finished retching. "That'll help some," he said, and closed one big hand around the back of the man's trousers, lifted him into the air as though he were a child, and, holding the kettle in his other hand, carried Titus Toomey out of the shed.

"Goddamn you, let go," Titus cursed between gasped breaths, his words still slurred and heavy with drink. Outside, Fargo set the kettle down again and lifted Titus Toomey high enough to fling him into the old trough, facedown. "Jesus, goddamn, aaaagh, Jesus," Titus gasped as Fargo pushed him under the water, held him there, then yanked him up sputtering and gasping for breath. He plunged the man into the water again, brought him up retching and gasping, did it again and again until finally Titus Toomey came up with some semblance of clarity in his eyes.

Fargo scooped a cup of the coffee from the kettle and thrust it at him. "Drink it, all of it," he said.

"Who the hell are you, mister?" Titus Toomey flared, and started to turn away. Fargo's hand closed around his neck, yanked him back, and he poured the coffee into the man's mouth. Toomey gagged and sputtered but most of the hot black liquid poured down his throat. Fargo held him again and poured another cup into him. He poured two more cups and half of each ran down the man's undershirt. When he released his grip, Toomey fell to the ground and retched violently.

Fargo stepped back and waited patiently until Titus Toomey stopped retching and shaking. Finally, the man lifted his head to peer at him with eyes that were confused but clear. "What'd I ever do to you, mister?" Titus asked.

"Nothing. Fact is, I've admired what I heard about

you, old man. You were one of the great guides," Fargo said.

"Who're you?" Titus Toomey asked.

"Name's Fargo, Skye Fargo."

Titus Toomey stared at him and a frown added one more crease to the lined face. "The one they call Trailsman?" he asked, and Fargo nodded. The man's frown deepened. "What in hell you come chasin' after me for?" he asked.

"Want some answers not out of a bottle," Fargo said.

The lined, weathered face took on caution. "What kind of answers?" Titus Toomey questioned.

"About what you told the major and why," Fargo said, and the caution turned to crafty fear.

"I don't want any trouble with Devereaux," the old man said. "He runs things around here. He could have me booted out of town."

"Last night I heard you call him a stupid-ass fool. Why?" Fargo asked harshly, and saw Titus Toomey's face draw in on itself. "You were a great guide once. Your courage come out of a bottle then too?" Fargo dug.

A flash of angry pride leaped in the weathered face. "Goddamn you, Fargo. I've forgotten more about courage than you young fellers know," Titus Toomey snapped.

"Prove it. Why'd you call Devereaux a stupid ass?" Fargo pressed.

Titus Toomey's cracked lips thinned for a moment as he gathered himself and his eyes lifted to meet Fargo's waiting gaze. "There's an Arapaho chief called Red Claw because he wears a big grizzly claw red with blood around his neck," Titus said. "He's important, vicious, and smart. Devereaux has his younger brother, Nokato, and two more braves, locked in the compound guardhouse."

Fargo heard the low whistle that escaped through his lips. "That explains all those troopers I saw on guard there," he murmured.

"A patrol blundered onto Nokato and the other two and got lucky and brought him back," Titus said. "When I heard they were holding him in the guard-house I went to Devereaux. I told him to hang the damn brother and do it quick." He paused, eyed Fargo with a querulous frown. "I don't have to give you reasons, I hope," he said.

"No, you don't," Fargo said. "I know the Indians. Something that's over with is over. They might hate more but they won't spill blood over something that can't be changed."

"But that damn fool wouldn't do it. He's waiting for a territory judge to arrive, hold a trial, and sentence the Arapaho to hanging all proper and legal," Titus said. "I told him that was the stupidest goddamn thing I ever heard of."

"He give you reasons?" Fargo queried.

"No, but of course he's got some damnfool rea-sons. He just called me a bloodthirsty, Indian-hating old drunk and had me thrown out," the old man said. "Maybe he'll give you his damn fool reasons. I don't even want to hear them."

Fargo saw the emptied, charred wagons in his thoughts. "Suddenly a lot of things begin to fit," he murmured.

"Don't they," Titus grunted.

"I'm going to have another talk with the major. It'll be like locking the barn door after the horse is gone. The damage is done already but maybe I can get him to listen to me."

"Maybe. You're not the town drunk."

"Neither are you, not for a while, at least," Fargo said, and the weathered face frowned up at him at once.

"What the hell's that mean?" Titus asked.

"It means you're going to stay off the sauce," Fargo snapped. "Things go the way I'm thinking they will, I'm going to need somebody who knows Indians besides myself, somebody who can trail and track and knows what signs mean."

"Forget it. It's been too long," Titus said, and turned away.

"Don't bullshit me, old man. You don't forget what's part of you. It's there inside you for always."

"Well, maybe I just don't want to. Maybe I've had my fill of it."

"I saw a fair number of youngsters around. Think they've had their fill of living?" Fargo slid at the old man.

Titus Toomey's eyes narrowed at him with shrewd and grudging appraisal. "Can you use a six-gun as well as you use words?" he asked.

"Better," Fargo said.

Titus surveyed the empty bottles strewn across the shed. "It'll be hard, too hard," he muttered.

"We'll start by throwing out all these reminders. That'll help."

"A habit's hard to break."

"Think of it this way, Titus Toomey. You break the habit or I'll break your neck," Fargo said evenly.

Titus peered hard at him. "Damn, if I don't think you mean that."

"I do."

Titus shrugged. "Well, that's as good a reason as I need."

Fargo turned and began to pick up old bottles as Titus looked on. He put them all into an old packing crate and dragged the crate outside. "You got any decent clothes?" he asked, eyeing the torn and stained undershirt and trousers.

A wry smile slid across the lined face. "Put away in a duffel bag. Funny, I've never touched them, never tried to sell any of them no matter how desperate I was for a bottle. Wonder why?"

"I'd guess because you couldn't cut away the past completely. You never let go all the way the way the real drunk does," Fargo said.

"Might just be so," Titus said, and he gave the Trailsman a sideways glance. "What's your stake in this, Fargo?" he asked.

Fargo let answers tumble through his mind and realized there was no single, overriding reason he could marshal. Molly swam into his thoughts, so did Bess Devereaux, as did the charred wagons and the children he'd glimpsed in town. And perhaps most of all, the sense of time racing headlong to disaster. It all came together to pull at him. "I'm here," he said. "And I can't see myself hightailing it. I figure I've no choice but to do what I can."

Titus nodded at the answer and Fargo swung onto the Ovaro. "Now what, young feller?" Titus asked.

"Clean yourself up and meet me outside Dolly's," Fargo said, and saw a wry smile crack the weathered lips.

"Testing me, are you?" Titus said.

"No, it's just a convenient spot to meet," Fargo said, and put the horse into a trot as Titus shuffled into the shed. He frowned in thought as he rode through town. He felt he'd reached Titus Toomey. The man still had pride in himself. But only time would tell, he knew. The bottle could be a deadly siren. Fargo neared the compound, slowed, and had just entered when he saw Bess Devereaux ride in with two troopers behind her. She brought her horse over to him as he dismounted.

"Daddy wouldn't let me go for a canter without an escort," she said with a trace of annoyance.

"Be glad—or do you just have a short memory?" Fargo said.

"They're not going to come close to town and the compound," she said.

"Don't bet on it," Fargo said. He walked on to the compound and heard her at his heels. "I'll announce myself, sonny," he said to the corporal as he strode past into the inner office. Devereaux looked up from behind his desk, startled but quickly pulling tolerant amusement into his face. Lieutenant Baker stood beside the desk, Fargo saw as he came to a halt.

"Another visit so soon, Fargo?" the major said.

"You forgot to mention something," Fargo growled.

"About holding the Arapahos?" Major Devereaux smiled.

"About holding the brother of a powerful Arapaho chief," Fargo corrected.

"You've been talking to the town drunk, it seems," the major said, and sat back in his chair.

"That town drunk knows more about the Indian than you'll ever learn," Fargo said. "This makes everything fit. All that talk about the Indians taking prisoners was bullshit and you know it."

The man drew an indignant glare into his face. "Not at all. I still believe that. Red Claw is retaliating, that's all, and that's to be expected."

"He's doing a lot more than retaliating, cousin," Fargo snapped.

"Such as?"

"I'm not sure but he's got something planned," Fargo said.

"I agree with the major," Lieutenant Baker put in. "Tragic as it is for the poor souls in the wagons, it's all pure retaliation. It'll blow over."

"Of course it will," the major said. "Meanwhile, I'm having the lieutenant take a detail and bring all

49

the families in the outlying areas into the compound until things settle down."

Fargo's glance took in Bess listening in the doorway and his lips bit down onto each other as he fastened his gaze on Devereaux again. "Tell me, why didn't you listen to Titus Toomey? Why didn't you hang Nokato the minute you brought him in?" he asked.

"It's important the Arapaho see that we do things according to law and order, after a proper, civilized trial and a proper sentencing," Devereaux said. "We must show an example."

Fargo frowned incredulously at the man. "You really think Red Claw gives a shit about white man's rules and laws?" he asked. "Jesus, why don't you read to him about little Red Riding Hood?"

The man's face hardened at once and he stood up. "I think I've heard quite enough from you, Mr. Fargo," he said stiffly.

"You're going to want to hear a lot more from me before this is over," Fargo said, and once more he strode out of the office. He passed Bess with a glance from eyes cold as an ice-bound lake. He'd reached the pinto outside when she hurried out, her face grave. He looked at the returning double column of troopers that filed into the compound. They'd ridden hard, Fargo saw, their horses lathered and weariness in each man's face. But they were alone, just as when they'd left in the morning. Bess brought her eyes up to Fargo's gaze, reluctant admission in the gray-blue orbs.

"You and Daddy, maybe you're both right," she said.

"How?" he asked harshly.

"You're right in practice, he's right in principle," she offered. "You're right about how things really turn out. He's right about the way they ought to be."

She was offering a compromise, her own intuition

pushing at her. But so was loyalty, years of admiration, and the bonds of blood. But he refused to soften truth for her. "Ought to be doesn't mean shit," he said harshly. "It's the way things are that counts, nothing else."

He saw the flash of pain touch her eyes as she turned away. He stayed silent. She'd have to face more pain, he was certain. She was about to have a crash course in harshness and he rode away as she disappeared into the building. Dusk began to sift itself down as he moved through the town and he was opposite the general store when he saw Molly come out, her neat, balanced figure hurrying toward him, breasts bouncing inside a dark-green dress with a square neck. Behind her, a slightly built man with serious, deep brown eyes and a storekeeper's apron wrapped around him hurried after her.

"This is Ed Kroger, Fargo," Molly introduced. "I told Ed about you." Fargo fastened a glance of quiet amusement on her and her lips tightened. "About how you're the Trailsman, the very best," she added and answered his glance. "Ed wants to hear what you think about things."

"Be honest with me, Fargo," the man said. "Are they all dead by now?"

"I'd guess not," Fargo said.

"But that stinkin' Arapaho plans to kill them, right?" Ed Kroger pressed.

"Maybe," Fargo said. "Or maybe use them to kill a lot more people."

"Can you help them, Fargo?" Ed Kroger asked.

"That depends," Fargo said.

"On what?" the man asked.

"Right now on Red Claw and Major Devereaux," Fargo answered. "I'll do whatever I think is best if I get the chance."

"Can't ask more than that," Ed Kroger said, and turned back to his store, his shoulders stooped as if he carried an invisible sack on them.

Fargo met Molly's grave gaze. "My rooms's at the back of the ground floor, behind the store," she said. "I don't care about being careful anymore. You come whenever you want, Fargo."

"Tomorrow night," he said, and she nodded and hurried back to the store as darkness fell over Owlshead. He went on to Dolly's place and halted as the thin-legged figure straightened up beside a post and came toward him. Titus Toomey wore a fringed buckskin jacket over a wool shirt and faded blue Levi's. On his hip, he carried a big Remington army revolver, single action with a brass trigger guard. He halted before Fargo almost sheepishly.

"Didn't hardly recognize you, Titus," Fargo commented.

"Neither did Dolly." Titus chuckled. "Things weren't too wrinkled, surprising. Got me a horse, good deep-chested mare from Sam Whitestone. Lots of wind to her. Sam always has extra horses cluttering up his place."

"Let's ride some," Fargo said, and Titus fetched the mare from the deep shadows at the other end of the hitching post. A good, sturdy horse indeed, Fargo noted. He led the way back through town, slowed as he saw Lieutenant Baker and his detail entering the compound with a group of families, most in buckboards and farm wagons, a few on horseback.

"Better late than never," Titus grunted as he followed Fargo on past the end of the compound and up to a low ridge that afforded a view of Owlshead to the left and the surrounding terrain in the pale moon's light.

"Talk to me, Titus," Fargo said. "Red Claw didn't take slaves. We both know that."

"We do," Titus grunted. "He took himself flesh-and-blood trading beads."

"Which way will he come?" Fargo asked, more to test the old man's wisdom than anything else.

Titus Toomey's eyes scanned the land in a slow circle. "That way, from the east," he said finally.

"With the sun at his back and in our eyes," Fargo agreed grimly. "He'll make us squint while we talk to him. Make your enemy nervous, in big ways and little ways. The Indian knows that's important." He let his eyes move over the land to the east. There was enough tree cover to let the Arapaho come within a hundred yards of the compound before being spotted. "We'll bed down over there," he said, and started toward a thick cluster of chestnut trees to the far side of the compound.

He nosed the pinto into the chestnut thicket, dismounted, and laid out his bedroll as Titus curled himself up against a slanted tree trunk. Fargo lay down, pulled off his clothes, and closed his eyes. The hard part was only beginning.

4

Fargo rose with the first pink streak of dawn and saw Titus stir, open his eyes, and blink. "Been a long time since I saw the dawn come up," the old guide said with a trace of wistfulness in his voice. Fargo used his canteen to wash, and when he swung onto the Ovaro, Titus pulled up on his brown mare and followed to where Fargo halted at the edge of the chestnuts. In the distance, he could see the lone sentry atop the stockade wall but he brought his gaze back to the line of trees to the east. When the sun began to peek around the edge of the far hills, he caught the movement in the trees and, moments later, watched the lone rider appear on a mostly white pony with a single brown patch on its rump.

The Indian, bare-chested, wore a tall eagle's feather standing up straight from a beaded headband. He rode slowly toward the stockade and Fargo saw the sentry spin to shout an alarm down into the compound. A half-dozen rifle-bearing troopers appeared in moments atop the stockade wall. The Indian continued to advance, walked his horse at a slow pace, and halted after he'd moved a few dozen yards closer to the compound. Suddenly, as if by magic, some fifteen horsemen appeared out of the trees, stretched in a single, horizontal line behind the lone horseman. They halted when he did to stay a dozen yards behind. Each sat with an arrow resting on a bowstring, except for the two end riders, Fargo noted. They carried army-issue Remington rifles.

The Indian on the white pony say unmoving and Fargo's eyes went to the compound. He guessed some six minutes had passed when he saw the gate swing open and two horses emerged, Devereaux on one, Lieutenant Baker on the other. Six more troopers followed them out, a half-dozen yards behind them. "Let's go," Fargo murmured, and spurred the Ovaro forward at a fast canter, Titus close behind. He crossed the distance at an angle and intercepted the two officers before they reached the Indian on the white pony. The major frowned in surprise as he pulled up alongside him.

"Where did you come from?" Devereaux asked.

"From inside those chestnuts," Fargo said.

"You expected this?" Devereaux asked

"More or less," Fargo said.

"Can you speak their tongue?" the major asked.

"Well enough. The Arapaho speak Algonkian, along with the Cheyenne, the Blackfoot, and half a dozen more Plains tribes. I'm best at Siouan but I can get along in Algonkian." He drew to a halt along with Devereaux and took in the Arapaho that sat unmoving on his pony. A huge grizzly claw hung from the Indian's neck on a hammered silver chain, the claw red with fresh blood. The Arapaho chief's face was as if carved of stone, a hook nose and high, flat cheekbones, eyes small bits of black coal that held only hate in them. "You are Red Claw," Fargo said.

The Indian barely nodded but his black eyes held on the big man on the Ovaro. "You are the one who saved the woman and killed two of my warriors," he said. "The others told me of you."

"The girl too. Killed two more of your braves, then," Fargo said with studied casualness. The Arapaho's face remained expressionless but Fargo saw the tiny flicker in the black eyes.

"Ask him what he wants," Devereaux said as Fargo's eyes stayed on the Indian.

"The chief of the soldiers wants to know why you come here," Fargo said.

"And you?" Red Claw asked.

"I know," Fargo grunted.

"Tell him," Red Claw said, and nodded toward the major.

"You are here. You talk," Fargo answered, and saw Red Claw turn his gaze on Major Devereaux. He spoke in short clusters of words, used his hands only twice to add emphasis in sign language. "Turn his brother and the others loose or he kills all of your people," Fargo translated. "One by one."

Fargo saw the anger tighten Devereaux's face. "He's got some goddamn nerve coming here with demands," the major spat out.

"He has," Fargo agreed. "And he's got two wagons and more of hostages. Your move."

"Tell him he can't blackmail me," Devereaux said.

"Good enough," Fargo said, and turned toward Red Claw.

"Wait," Devereaux bit out. "Maybe we should bargain some more."

"He's not going to bargain and he's not going to play games with you," Fargo said.

"Good God, man, I can't make a decision like this on the spur of the moment," Devereaux protested.

"You show weakness and you're lost," Fargo said.

"Dammit, I need time," the major said, his voice a hoarse cry. Fargo considered for a moment as he cursed silently. Red Claw's black-bits eyes had already speared through Devereaux, he was certain, taken the measure of the man in his own way. When he turned to the Arapaho chief, he used sign language in addition to his words to make certain he'd not be misunderstood.

"The chief of the soldiers cannot answer now. He must hold council with his warriors," Fargo said. It was an answer the Arapaho would understand, he knew.

The Indian thought for a moment as his stone face showed no change. "Tomorrow, at the sun's rise, I will return," he said. Fargo relayed the answer to Devereaux, who cursed silently.

"Wait a minute," Lieutenant Baker cut in. "How do we know they're not all dead already? He could be trying to pull a fast one."

Fargo sought the Arapaho chief's stony glare. "Maybe Red Claw lies," he said. "Maybe his captives are all dead already."

The stone face showed a flicker of expression, anger tightening his lips, Fargo saw in satisfaction. The Indian jerked his arm up and two more riders burst from the trees. They held a woman between them as they rode, and when they skidded to a halt, they let her down to the ground but kept hold of her wrists. "Good God, it's Emily Kroger," Major Devereaux said.

The woman had a round face, Fargo saw, that was now drawn and haggard with terror, normally soft brown eyes that stared wildly, her hair wildly unkempt and her blue traveling dress ripped in two places.

"Please, give them whatever they want," she gasped out. "Oh, God, please."

"Are the others all still alive?" Devereaux asked.

"Yes, yes, so far," Emily Kroger said. "But they keep telling us what they're going to do to us. Don't let them, oh, please don't let them."

Red Claw moved one hand upward and the two braves yanked the woman into the air between them, held her between their horses as they turned and raced back into the trees with her. Fargo saw Major Devereaux spit curses at the Arapaho chief. "You savage bastard," he rasped, and Red Claw had to understand the message if not the words, but his face remained impassive.

"Can we stall him?" Lieutenant Baker asked. Titus gave him the answer with a derisive sound.

Devereaux's lips twitched in his strained face. "Tell him I'll give him his answer tomorrow morning," he said, and Fargo relayed the message. The Arapaho chief turned and calmly rode away while, in unison, the line of warriors vanished into the trees as silently as they had appeared. With the lieutenant at his heels, the major wheeled his mount and hurried back to the compound and Fargo and Titus followed slowly. When they neared the gates, Fargo saw the large cluster of townspeople gathered there. Red Claw's demands had to have been heard by the six troopers standing by. They'd not be kept secret, Fargo was certain, but he rode quickly past the townspeople and halted only when he reached Dolly's place.

Titus followed him inside and Dolly greeted them with curiosity. "Coffee, hot and strong," Fargo ordered, and the woman disappeared into the kitchen.

"By day's end the whole town will be knocking on Devereaux's door," Titus said, and Fargo nodded, took one of the two mugs of coffee Dolly brought out. He let the bracing, hot brew make its way down inside him as his lips pursed.

"He'll never stand up to them," Fargo said.

"Not unless you can give some backbone," Titus grunted between sips.

"I'll speak my piece. I can't do more than that," Fargo said. Titus nodded grimly and drained his mug. "Let's ride some," Fargo said, and got to his feet. Outside, as he started slowly through Owlshead, he saw that the word had already spread. Clusters of men and women spoke in hushed tones and even those hurrying about their business did so with grave faces. When they reached the general store, he saw the door fly open and Molly rush out and he reined to a halt. Her neat, balanced figure was encased in a tight-bodiced tan dress and she'd fluffed her hair out at the bottom. " 'Morning, Molly. You look mighty pretty," Fargo commented.

"I wish I felt pretty," she said. "There's going to be a meeting at the compound at four o'clock. Everyone's concerned that Major Devereaux understands what he has to do. I hope you'll be there."

"Why?"

'You know Indians. So's you can add your voice," Molly said, and he caught the wry glance Titus tossed at him. He nodded and moved the Ovaro forward and swore silently as he did. Titus slowed when they reached the blacksmith shop. "The mare's got a loose shoe in her right forefoot," he said. "It'll take fifteen minutes, maybe."

"I'll wait for you at the end of town," Fargo said, and rode on. He'd almost reached the end of town when he saw the flash of honey-wheat hair coming toward him at the reins of a buckboard. Bess Devereaux reined to a halt and he saw the bags of groceries and cotton goods inside the buckboard. A little smile toyed with her lips as she gave him a sideways, appraising glance.

"The world is full of surprises," she said. "Here I'd assumed your little playmate in the woods was one of Dolly's girls. It seems I was wrong."

"Is that so," Fargo said evenly.

"I recognized her in the general store, even with her clothes on," Bess said waspishly.

"Careful, honey," Fargo growled.

"A respectable woman of the community frolicking naked in the woods," she said. "You seem able to bring out the best in a woman, Fargo. Or is it the worst?" Her little laugh was taunting and condescending.

"You're welcome to find out anytime you like," he said.

"I'm sure you'd really enjoy that," Bess Devereaux said with disdainful superiority in her tone.

"No," Fargo said.

"No?" She frowned.

"But you would," he remarked, and saw the instant flare of anger in her eyes as he rode on. He heard her snap the reins sharply and the buckboard roll on with a rattle of wheels. When he reached the end of town, he halted and had only a few minutes' wait as Titus came along.

"Passed Devereaux's daughter driving a buckboard like she was in some kind of race," Titus said. "You wouldn't know anything about that, would you?"

"Let's ride," Fargo said.

"Thought so." Titus chuckled and followed him out of town. Fargo took the first set of hills at a canter and slowed at the second ridgeline.

"You go east, I'll circle west. We'll meet back here

in a few hours," he said, and Titus nodded and turned his mare eastward. The old guide didn't need more words, Fargo knew, and he began the slow circle to the west. His eyes scanned the ground as he rode, lifted ocassionally to peer into the tree cover, and returned to the marks and tracks that formed their own book for him. It was slow, painstaking riding with the kind of concentration that used up energy. The sun had moved across the afternoon sky when he finally completed the wide circle at the ridge and saw Titus coming toward him. Fargo questioned with a glance as the old guide drew to a halt.

"They've been real smart. Lots of tracks, new and old, too many to read," Titus said.

"Yes, they've crossed back and forth over and over with each trip they take. Very cagey."

"But they all edge north, little by little."

"Just what I picked up," Fargo agreed. "They're coming from someplace at the foot of Shadow Mountain, I'd guess."

"Got to be there," Titus concurred. "Far enough yet close enough."

Fargo glanced up at the sun. "Not anything more we can do today. Let's get back," he said, and put the pinto into a fast canter. When he reached Owlshead, he rode on to the compound and saw the crowd that had already gathered in front of the major's quarters. A ring of troopers looked on uneasily and Fargo saw Lieutenant Baker standing to one side. He found Molly standing alongside Ed Kroger as he made his way around the edge of the crowd to the front row. He dismounted, Titus beside him, and drifted to one side of the headquarters building as Major Devereaux came outside, Bess following him, and Fargo saw her stay in the background as she leaned against a post.

Devereaux surveyed the crowd as he halted on the top step of the headquarters building. "I know why you're here, of course," he began. "You've come to know what I'm going to do about that savage's demands."

A big man with a green plaid shirt and a black beard spoke up from the center of the crowd. "We're here to say there's only one thing to do," he corrected.

Devereaux, Fargo saw, gazed at the crowd with just the proper mixture of sympathy and firm authority. "I'm as filled with agony as all of you are and I churn inside when I think of giving in to that arrogant savage," he said. "But I don't have a choice, it seems."

"That's right," a woman called out. "You don't give him his brother back and all our loved ones will be killed."

"My Sarah was on those wagons," another man said. "I'm not letting her die for some damn Indian."

A chorus of agreement swelled at once and Devereaux held up his hand. "I can't turn my back on all your loved ones. I'll have to give into his demands. Much as I hate it," the major said. "All of you who agree, raise your hands." Fargo watched the sea of hands explode into the air along with the murmur of sound and his lips were a thin line. "Then we're all in this together," Devereaux said. "And I'll get your loved ones back for you."

Fargo spat silently. The man was playing the reluctant savior for all it was worth. Ed Kroger's voice cut into his thoughts. "I didn't see Mr. Fargo raise his hand," the man called out.

"You didn't," Fargo said. "Because you can't do this. You can't give in to Red Claw."

He saw Devereaux frown at him as the swell of anger rose from the crowd. "What the hell do you mean, mister?" a man called out. "There's nothing else we can do."

"You can tell him to go to hell," Fargo said, his eyes on the major.

"And condemn our families? What the hell kind of talk is that?" someone else answered.

Fargo turned to the crowd, his eyes sweeping the men and women with unwavering firmness. "It's hard talk. Rotten talk. But it's true," he said. "You give in to Red Claw and you're condemning yourselves, you're condemning every wagon train that heads west and every settlement and every family in the territory. Once he sees that all he has to do is take hostages to get what he wants, you're all finished. Word will spread to the other tribes damn quickly. You'll be feeding a fire that'll never stop."

"All I care about is getting my Sarah back alive," a man called out.

"Same here. I want my daughters back," another voice chimed in.

"And my Tom," a woman added.

"It won't go the way you think," Fargo said. "Not once Red Claw sees he has the upper hand."

"Hell, Fargo, that Indian isn't holding one of yours," Ed Kroger shouted. "I'll bet you wouldn't talk the same way if he were."

"Probably not," Fargo conceded. "And I'd be as wrong as you are now."

"We're not listenin' to any more of that kind of talk," the man in the green plaid shirt boomed out. "You just get us our families, back, Major," he said, and angry agreement swelled from the crowd.

"I'll do everything I can. Count on it," Devereaux told them. "Now go home and pray." Muttering, the crowd turned and began to walk through the compound gates and down the main street of town as night descended. Lieutenant Baker ordered his troopers to their barracks and Fargo saw Titus climb onto the mare.

'See you back at Dolly's," the old guide said, and rode away. Fargo felt Devereaux's eyes on him and turned to the man, his gaze taking in Bess Devereaux nearby.

"You're wrong, real wrong," Fargo said.

"You heard those people," Devereaux flung back. "You've got your nerve telling me to let them down. I'm not here to turn my back on them. I'm here to protect them."

"You're here to do what's right, for all settlers everywhere, for the whole damn Colorado territory, and you're not doing that. You're taking the easy way out," Fargo shot back, and saw Devereaux's face grow flushed at once.

"That'll be quite enough from you, mister. You just be here come morning when Red Claw shows up. I want you to see I'm doing the right thing with your own eyes," the major said. Fargo turned from the man and strode to the Ovaro as Devereaux disappeared into his quarters.

"That was rotten cruel," Fargo heard the voice say, and saw Bess coming up to him, gray-blue eyes blazing. "Accusing him of taking the easy way out. How dare you? You heard those people. They want their loved ones back. That's all they care about."

"Yes, and they can't see anything else but that. I understand that. They're supposed to feel that way. I expect that of them."

"But not of Father."

"That's right," Fargo snapped back. "I expect something more of an officer. I expect him to do what's right, not what's popular."

"You expect him to sacrifice the hostages Red Claw's holding?" Bess frowned.

"If that's what has to be done. It'd take a hell of a lot of guts, a lot more than he has." Fargo grimaced. Bess Devereaux's hand came up in a short arc but he caught her wrist before the blow struck his cheek.

"Damn you," she hissed. He forced her arm down slowly and took his fingers from around her wrist. "Compassion isn't weakness," she flung at him.

"No, but it makes a good hiding place for it," he said, and climbed onto the Ovaro.

"It's not your decision to make. Talk's easy and then you can just ride off," Bess said, and he caught the break in her voice.

"None of us are going to just ride off, not now," he said almost sadly, and turned the Ovaro away. He rode from the compound and through town to the dance hall, dismounted, and went inside. Once again, the place was more empty than full and he saw Dolly sitting with Titus at one of the tables.

"First and last for the night," Titus said, raising his glass.

"You better mean it," Fargo grunted. "I'll be back later for you. We'll bed down in the chestnuts again." Titus nodded and Fargo strode from the saloon. He led the Ovaro down the street toward the general store. It'd be good to lose himself in Molly's warm and willing arms, an oasis of pleasure to wipe away the problems for a little while. He could feel the touch of her against him in his thoughts as he reached the darkened store, went around to the back where he saw the light on behind a curtained window.

He knocked softly on the door and Molly opened, her neat shape wrapped in a dark blue cotton robe that nonetheless curved around the swell of her breasts

But she glared at him, unmoving, no welcome in her face. "I wondered if you'd have the nerve to show up," she said. "I suppose I should've known better."

Fargo frowned. "What're you talking about?"

"After the way you behaved at that meeting," Molly said. "I never heard such a cold, insensitive attitude. I couldn't believe my ears."

"I said what had to be said," Fargo growled. "I don't see where it ought to affect us."

"That's too bad because it certainly affects me. I can't stop thinking of how unfeeling you were. Maybe I just never saw that part of you but right now I can't be close to anyone with that little regard for others. I expected more than such callousness from you," Molly said.

"And I expected more than this kind of blind, weak-kneed dumbness from you," Fargo shot back.

"Good night," Molly snapped.

"Same to you," Fargo said before she slammed the door shut. He turned as disappointment and anger bubbled inside him. Damn fool girl, he growled silently. She couldn't see any more clearly than the rest of them, her emotions all caught up with friendships and sympathies. He should've expected as much, he realized. But he hadn't and the wanting would take a spell to wind down. He rode from the south end of town into the clear night, the moon pale, and he'd gone only a few dozen yards when he saw the horse alongside a box elder. Honey-wheat hair flashed atop the figure standing next to the mount as the moonlight glinted on it. He steered the pinto over and swung to the ground. "Your pa know you're out here?" he asked.

"No, he went to bed. I wanted to get some air. I didn't plan to go any further than here," Bess Devereaux said. He saw her lips take on the hint of a smile as she studied him. "I didn't expect to see you here," she commented.

"Meaning what?" he asked.

"I saw you going around to the back of the general store as I rode by," she said. "Trouble in paradise? No roll in the woods tonight? Or anywhere else?" The smile grew wider, became cool, taunting.

"You've got a lot of wasp in your tongue, haven't you?" Fargo said.

She shrugged. "I'm enjoying the moment," she said.

"I might as well too," Fargo said, reached out and closed one hand around her waist, and pulled her to him. His mouth pressed down on hers, found sweet-tasting, soft lips that yielded as much from surprise as response. The warmth of her pressed against him, soft breasts pushing into his chest, a small, firm waist under his hand. She tried to make her lips firm but he pressed harder and felt her soften for an instant before she tore from his grasp.

"You've got your nerve," Bess Devereaux said. "I'll be no substitute."

"Didn't expect that," Fargo said calmly. "Just sampling."

"Try Dolly's," Bess snapped, and climbed onto her horse. She rode off at a fast canter, not glancing back, but he knew she heard his laugh and he waited till she was gathered up by the darkness in the streets of town. He rode slowly back to the dance hall, then, picked up Titus, who had kept his word about one drink, and rode north out beyond the compound to the cluster of chestnuts.

"I'll stay with Devereaux come morning. You know what you're to do," he said to the old guide as he lay down.

"Yep," Titus grunted, and stretched his thin legs out, his head against a small mound of earth.

"Hang back. Don't take any chances. When you lose ground cover, turn back," Fargo said.

"Got it," Titus said. "Maybe Devereaux will get lucky. Maybe that damn Arapaho will take his brother back and back off."

Fargo thought of Red Claw's hard-stone face, the arrogance in it and the hate in the black coal eyes. "Maybe you'll get fat by morning," he said to Titus, and closed his eyes. He drew sleep around himself. The dawn would arrive all too soon, he knew.

5

The pink-gray morning light had just touched the earth when he woke and saw Titus vanishing through the trees, leading the brown mare behind him. Fargo sat up, stretched, and finally rose to his feet and Titus was no longer in sight. He listened and smiled. The old fox knew how to move silently through the woods. Fargo washed, unhurriedly, drew his gunbelt on, and led the Ovaro to the edge of the chestnuts where he could see the compound. When the morning sun rose over the mountains, he saw Devereaux ride from the compound, Lieutenant Baker at his side and the six troopers behind. Fargo climbed onto the Ovaro and rode out to meet the major, casting a glance along the line of trees to his right.

Devereaux drew a halt as Fargo came up to him, his gaze scanning the trees. "How do you plan on doing it?" Fargo asked.

"An exchange, of course," the major snapped. Fargo started to ask more but pulled questions back as the lone figure on the white pony came out of the trees, riding fast. Red Claw carried a lance this time, he saw, decorated on one side with coup feathers. "Where are the others?" Devereaux whispered as the Indian neared.

"In the trees. Count on it," Fargo said. "He's cagey. He won't do the same thing twice."

The Arapaho came to an abrupt halt, his black eyes fastened on Devereaux. Fargo saw the major try to cover the nervousness in his face with disdainful authority and knew that Red Claw saw through him with real contempt. "Tell him I will exchange his brother and the other two braves for the hostages he holds," the major said.

The Indian's glance went to Fargo, cold waiting in his eyes. "The major will give you Nokato and the others. You will give him those you hold as prisoner," Fargo said. Red Claw made a gesture, his face impassive. "He wants to know when," Fargo said to Devereaux.

"Now, if he wants," the major said, and Fargo relayed the answer. Red Claw considered for a moment and finally grunted his reply.

"An hour before sundown, at the edge of the trees," Fargo translated. Devereaux nodded and the Arapaho wheeled his pony around and raced away.

"Sneaking, cunning bastard," Fargo muttered after the disappearing Arapaho, and Devereaux frowned at him. "He's going to pull something."

"Nonsense. He's undoubtedly hidden the hostages someplace. He needs time to get them and bring them here," Devereaux said.

"Not that much time," Fargo grunted.

"No hostages, no exchanges. I'm sure he realizes that," the major said as he started back to the compound. "You just have a poor attitude, Fargo."

"That's a fact," Fargo said, and sent the pinto on as the others turned into the compound. He glimpsed Bess by the gate in her gray skirt and white blouse and looking coolly austere. He nodded to her and she

70

flashed a narrowed glance back as he rode on into Owlshead, where he halted at the saloon and went inside. Dolly had a mug of coffee on the table for him, he saw, and he sank into a chair.

"Obliged," he said, and took a long sip of the hot brew.

"Saw you coming," she said. "Where's Titus?"

"Out being a bird dog, a careful one, I hope," Fargo said between sips, and he saw the question in Dolly's eyes. "It's done," he growled. "And it's opened the doors to hell."

"Any way of shutting them again?" Dolly asked, and he gave her a long, thoughtful stare.

"That'll depend," Fargo said. "On how greedy Red Claw gets and how lucky we get." He finished the coffee, rose, and walked from the saloon with the grimness draped around him like an invisible cloak. He took the Ovaro out of town to the chestnuts and sank to the ground in a shade spot, stretched out, and watched the morning slowly slide into noon. Anxiousness began to stab at him and he sat up when he spied the horse come into sight with the straw-thin rider in the saddle. He felt the relief rush over him with surprising force. He'd come to like Titus Toomey for the inner strengths he'd shown and respect him for his trail-wise sagacity.

Titus rode into the trees and slid wearily from the mare to fold his reedy frame onto a soft place. "We were right yesterday. They headed straight for Shadow Mountain," he said. "I tailed them a good way until they slowed and began looking back. I figured they'd caught wind of me or were just being smart. Either way, I took cover and stayed there until they went on. I'd guess their camp wasn't more than a mile or two on."

"Good work, Titus," Fargo said. "Devereaux's going

to exchange Nokato for the hostages an hour before sundown. Red Claw's choice of time."

Titus made a wry sound. "Smart redskin, that one. He'll have the darkness covering his trail when they ride back," the old guide said. "And Devereaux still feels he's made a fine bargain."

"The fool," Fargo spat out. "He thinks Red Claw's going to act like an officer and a gentleman." He rose and went to his saddlebag and brought out some strips of beef jerky wrapped in oilskin. "Let's eat some. There's nothing to do now but wait," he said, and Titus took one of the strips and began to chew one end of it.

"I stopped waiting a long time ago," Titus said. "Feels funny to be doing it again."

"Why?" Fargo asked, and drew a quizzical glance. "Why'd Titus Toomey become the town drunk?" he continued.

"It all became too much one day, all the killing and hating and ravaging. Seems I was bringing folks out to be killed or become killers," Titus said. "I made the mistake of getting close to a family with three little boys. They went and got themselves massacred because they didn't listen to me."

"Wasn't your fault, then," Fargo commented.

"Not that but I brought them out here. Maybe they'd still be alive if I hadn't."

"Somebody else would have," Fargo said.

"Likely so but that's reason talk and it doesn't matter much when you're torn up inside. I figured I'd had all I wanted to see of the world and a bottle helps shut everything out. Gets to be a nice habit, sort of like floating on your own cloud."

"And I wrecked that all for you," Fargo said.

"I'll decide whether I'll thank you or tell you to go to hell when it's over," Titus said.

"Fair enough," Fargo said, and leaned back and closed his eyes. He dozed and listened to the yellow warblers sing in the trees until the sun began to slide toward the horizon. He rose and saw Titus come awake at once. "Time to see which way the ax is going to fall," Fargo said, and the old man pushed to his feet and climbed onto the brown mare. Fargo rode from the cluster of chestnuts and saw the major, Lieutenant Baker at his side again, emerge from the compound gate. Behind him, six troopers rode herd on three Arapaho. Fargo crossed the ground and the major slowed as he reached him, the line of trees a hundred yards on. Fargo's eyes went to the first in line of the three Arapahos. Nokato, contempt and disdain in his face, was younger than Red Claw but had the chief's hook nose in a thinner, weaker face, his frame without the power of his brother's body. Bare-chested, he wore only an elkhide breechclout and his mouth curled in a sneer of bravado. The other two braves were ordinary looking, slender figures, uneasiness in their bony features.

Major Devereaux acknowledged Fargo's arrival with a curt nod and continued on toward the trees. He halted a scant dozen yards from the first line of box elders, and moments later, Red Claw rode slowly out of the forest. Fargo saw his eyes immediately go to his younger brother. Six warriors appeared behind the Arapaho chief and rode forward to form a semicircle around him. Red Claw's gesture was unmistakable. Release Nokato, it said, and Devereaux frowned.

"Tell him when he releases the hostages," the major barked, and Fargo transmitted the message. Red Claw moved one arm and another two braves on horseback appeared, shepherding three hostages on foot, one a middle-aged woman, one a young girl, and the other a youth Fargo guessed to be in his twenties. The Indians halted and the three figures rushed toward the soldiers. The woman stumbled, almost fell, but the man caught her and helped her to keep going.

"Let the damn redskins go," Major Devereaux ordered through the side of his mouth. The troopers pulled away from the three braves and Nokato led the other two in their charge toward Red Claw. Fargo saw Devereaux's eyes peering into the trees; the major was waiting for the rest of the hostages to stream out. When Red Claw began to turn away, a frown of consternation and a flash of sudden panic crossed the major's face. "Wait. Where are the others?" he shouted, and glanced at Fargo. "Tell him to wait," he said.

Fargo swore softly. The Arapaho chief needed some sign of strength and purpose. He'd already dismissed Devereaux's words. Fargo's hand closed around the Colt, drew it from its holster, and fired in one quick, smooth motion. The bullet slammed into the ground inches in front of Red Claw's pony. Fargo saw the other Arapahos instantly lift their bows, arrows in place, but Red Claw halted and turned his pony halfway around. Fargo met the black-coal eyes that bored into him with unwavering firmness.

"The others," Fargo said.

Red Claw held up three fingers and made a gesture in sign language.

"What's he saying?" Devereaux asked.

"You gave him three, he gives you three," Fargo answered.

"Goddammit, that wasn't the agreement and he knows it," Devereaux shouted angrily. "It was Nokato for our people." Fargo nodded but Nokato and the other two braves were gone, vanished into the trees, and he swore under his breath. "I expected to see the rest of our people walk out of those trees," Devereaux said. "Tell him that."

"He knows what you expected. He counted on it," Fargo said grimly.

"We had an agreement, dammit. You tell him that," the major said, and Fargo spoke to the Arapaho chief in terse, curt tones. Red Claw answered, his face expressionless.

"He changed it," Fargo said to Devereaux, and watched angry frustration flush the man's face.

"He can't do that. Tell him I thought he understood about agreements, that he had some damn sense of honor," the major exploded.

Fargo grunted and spit the words at Red Claw he knew would reach the Indian. "Red Claw does not keep his word," he said.

The stone-faced expression changed for an instant, a brief flash of contempt crossing his wide-cheekboned face. "The white man speaks of not keeping his word?" Red Claw asked, and spat on the ground. Fargo swore inwardly again as he passed the reply to Devereaux.

"Damn arrogant savage," Devereaux muttered.

"Arrogant but accurate," Fargo grunted.

"The other hostages, I want to know about the other hostages," Devereaux shouted, and Fargo turned to Red Claw, spoke again to him, and turned the short answer back to Devereaux.

"He'll give you his answers on the other hostages come morning," Fargo said.

"I won't stand still for this," the major flared.

"You'll stand still for it or there won't be any other hostages to talk about. He made that clear to me," Fargo said grimly.

"No, dammit, he can't do this," Devereaux shouted, but Red Claw turned his back on him and sent the white pony toward the trees, the gesture one of infinite disdain. The meeting was finished, it said, and the other warriors followed their chief into the trees.

Devereaux's frustrated anger had to find a target as he spun his mount around and headed back toward the compound. "You expected this, didn't you?" he spat at Fargo.

"Just the music, not the words," Fargo returned as he rode to the compound, where the throng surged around the three freed hostages, embracing, welcoming, asking questions about the others. Ed Kroger stood to one side, his face wreathed in worry and disappointment, and Molly waited nearby. Devereaux reined to a halt and Fargo saw the crowd grow still as they heard the major's question flung at him.

"You've any thoughts about tomorrow, Fargo?" Devereaux asked.

"Only that he's got all the cards now," Fargo said.

"Nonsense. I was wrong in expecting him to keep his word. I know better now. He won't trick me again. I promise you," the major said, and Fargo flicked a glance at Bess as she listened, her eyes on him.

"He won't have to," Fargo said.

"Meaning what?" the major snapped.

Fargo frowned at the man. "You still don't understand, do you?" he said, not keeping the bitter incredulousness out of his voice.

"I understand he can't ask much more of anything. He has his brother back. That was his main prize. Whatever he comes up with now, I'll certainly handle. I think he just wants to milk this for all he can, make himself look big to his people," Devereaux said.

Fargo bit his lips shut, turned the Ovaro, and started to walk the horse on with Titus beside him. He'd gone only a few yards when he heard Bess call and he halted as she hurried after him. "I want to talk to you," she said severely. "Alone. Where?"

"Later, the end of town," he said. "Give me time to have a drink." She nodded and abruptly strode away.

He put the pinto into a trot until he drew up at Dolly's, hitched the horse to the post, and went inside, Titus a few paces behind him.

"Bourbon," he said, and surveyed the few patrons at the bar. Dolly came toward him in her evening blond wig as he sat down with Titus and she made a face.

"I hear it's not over," Dolly said.

"Not by a long shot." Titus sniffed. "Don't expect business to pick up any."

"Thanks," Dolly said, and brought the drinks to the table. Titus raised his glass to Fargo.

"Here's to trouble," he said, and the big man nodded as he took a long pull of his bourbon. "What's the Devereaux girl nosing around for?" Titus asked.

"Help for her pa," Fargo answered. "I feel sorry for her. It hurts to see an idol crumble."

"You think she sees that?" Titus questioned.

"Not yet. She won't let herself. She cares too much for him. She'll cling to admiration, blood ties, loyalty, to wanting to believe in him. But she's smart and her head won't let her heart run away with her."

"Meaning?" Dolly interjected.

"She's going to be torn up inside," Fargo said. "She won't be able to look away forever." He finished his bourbon, rose and strode from the saloon, and felt the grimness curled inside his stomach. Outside, he rode to the end of town, dismounted, and soon heard the sharp sound of a horse's hooves pounding into the ground at a hard canter. Bess Devereaux rode into sight, reined to a sharp halt, and swung to the ground and he enjoyed the way her breasts swayed in unison.

"I want to know what you meant before," she demanded. "What doesn't he understand?"

"Does it matter now?" Fargo asked.

"Why wouldn't it?" Bess demanded.

"Because it's done. That's what he doesn't understand. He thinks it's still all bargain and bluster, but it's not. The damage is done. He gave in and sent out the signals. Take hostages and get what you want," Fargo answered.

"He's saving lives," Bess flung back.

"Maybe and maybe not for long. And if so, how many others are going to pay the price? How many others will become hostages, their lives turned into bargaining chips?" Fargo pressed. "Red Claw won't let it rest at this. Neither will the other tribes once word spreads. Unless it's stopped now," he added.

"You said it's too late to stop," Bess countered.

"He's got one more chance in the morning," Fargo said. "But he won't take it."

"Because he's doing what he thinks is right," she flared. "Not because he's weak."

"You trying to convince me or yourself?" Fargo asked.

"Go to hell, Fargo," she snapped, pulled herself onto her horse, and threw him another glare. "You're wrong this time. You'll see," she insisted.

"I hope so," Fargo said evenly, and watched her longish breasts bounce as she sent the horse into a hard canter. He drew a deep sigh as he pulled himself onto the Ovaro and rode to the stand of chestnuts. He was nearly asleep when Titus rode in and settled down nearby.

"The girl come asking?" he muttered.

"She did, trying to look away from the stirrings inside her," Fargo answered. "Only it's too late now."

"Never could stand feeling helpless," Titus said. "But I sure do feel that now."

"Get some shut-eye. We can't even make plans until we see what Red Claw does come morning," Fargo said, and heard Titus grunt agreement and turn on his side. Fargo drew sleep around himself, refusing to speculate any longer on the inevitable.

When morning came he woke, washed, and waited for Titus to join him at a little stream behind where they'd slept. The sun had come up when he rode from the chestnuts and saw the compound gate swing open. Devereaux came out first, Lieutenant Baker behind him, and Fargo frowned as he saw the four columns of troopers follow the two officers.

"Hell, he's just about turned out the whole regiment," Titus breathed.

"He wants to impress Red Claw with a show of force," Fargo said.

"Shit," Titus muttered. "He doesn't know the difference between strength and force."

Devereaux rode up to where Fargo came to a halt not far from the line of trees, raised his arm, and the four columns of troopers reined up smartly. "There'll be no more tricks this time," the major said.

"I don't expect Red Claw's got any tricks in mind," Fargo said, and drew a sharp frown from Devereaux.

"What do you think he has in mind?" the man queried.

"To take you apart, little by little. You gave him a start. He'll do the rest," Fargo said.

"He'll find out differently. So will you, Fargo," Devereaux said, and Fargo watched him firm his lips and jut his jaw forward. He was, Fargo decided, not unlike an actor who had mastered all the right poses and expressions to play his role. Perhaps five minutes passed when the white pony emerged from the trees, alone, not another rider in sight. Red Claw rode toward Devereaux and the troopers with a calm, expressionless demeanor, and when he halted, his black-coal eyes moved disdainfully across the assembled regiment. He turned his gaze on Fargo and spoke in quick, stone-hard sentences.

"You can have the rest of the hostages alive for one hundred and fifty rifles and ammunition," Fargo translated.

"What?" Devereaux frowned.

"A hundred and fifty rifles," Fargo repeated. "No rifles and he kills the hostages."

"That bastard," Devereaux spit out. "He's got his damn nerve."

"He wants an answer now, no waiting," Fargo added. Devereaux, his mouth a thin, tight line, looked back to the compound where it seemed almost the entire town had lined up to wait. The major brought his eyes back to Fargo and he drew compassion into his face.

"Sacrifice their loved ones for some rifles? I can't do that. I've no choice," the major said.

"Tell it to them, not me," Fargo growled.

"My God, Fargo, sacrificing people for a few cases of rifles? How would that look in a report back to Washington?" the major said.

"You won't have to worry about it if you keep giving in," Fargo said.

"I'll handle Red Claw when the time comes," Devereaux said.

"Arming a hundred and fifty Arapahos with rifles will make them one damn powerful force," Fargo said.

"But untrained. My troopers are disciplined and trained fighting men," Devereaux said, and Fargo cast a glance at Lieutenant Baker. The lieutenant's young, smooth face carried discomfort in it. Fargo turned back to Devereaux.

"Say no. Get some backbone, dammit. Don't pile one wrong on another," he said.

"Tell that cunning savage I'll give him his rifles,"

Devereaux said. "But tell him he won't trick me again. I want to see every hostage free before he gets one rifle."

Fargo heard the bitterness in the sigh that escaped him as he relayed the major's words to the Arapaho chief. Red Claw turned on his pony and waved one arm. In moments, a dozen warriors on horseback appeared on a distant rise of land, the hostages on foot between them. They halted and kept their prisoners in line as Red Claw barked words. "Get the rifles," Fargo translated, and Devereaux turned to the lieutenant.

"A hundred and fifty rifles will be six crates, the ammo boxes another six. Take fifteen men and get the equipment. On the double," the major snapped, and the lieutenant went off to gather the detail. Devereaux's eyes went to Fargo with disdain. "You're going to find yourself all wrong this time, Fargo," he said. Fargo made no reply as he stared beyond Devereaux to the compound and caught the flash of honey-wheat hair among those gathered outside the gate. As he watched, Lieutenant Baker and his detail rode from the gate, each crate of rifles carried by two troopers riding in pairs.

Devereaux turned to the main body of his troops with confident triumph. "Stretch out and form two columns about ten yards apart," he ordered, and Fargo watched the troopers execute the order with quick precision. Lieutenant Baker's detail deposited the rifles and ammunition boxes at one end of the facing columns and Devereaux turned to Fargo. "Tell that arrogant savage to bring the hostages between the troopers. When they're safely through, he can pick up the rifles," the major said. Fargo nodded, translated the message to Red Claw, and the Indian motioned to the braves on the distant rise. They began to herd their captives down the slope, and as they did so Fargo saw at least fifty more warriors emerge from the trees to form a line behind Red Claw, arrows poised on their bowstrings. Devereaux's frown had alarm in it. "What's he up to?" he muttered.

"Just his way of warning you not to pull off anything tricky," Fargo said, his eyes on the hostages as they hurried toward the two lines of waiting troops, grateful relief trying to push the fear from their faces. He saw Emily Kroger in the first line, flanked by two younger women, and as the small group of weary, frightened figures began to move between the lines of troops, the dozen Arapaho shepherding them came to a halt.

"Dismount," Lieutenant Baker ordered his detail. "Help those people to the compound." Red Claw looked on impassively as his braves began to carry the rifle crates away, and when they moved the last box of ammunition into the trees, the Arapaho chief turned his face to the big man with the lake-blue eyes.

"Even an eagle cannot fly with a weasel on its back," he said, words that were a backhanded compliment, words of recognition and of warning.

"Some eagles are fools," Fargo answered, and Red Claw acknowledged the reply with a flicker of his black-coal eyes as he slowly rode into the trees. Fargo turned his horse and hurried back to the compound with Titus. He halted at the scene of joyful embraces and jubilation, picked out Molly, and received a glance of smug satisfaction from her as she stood between Emily and Ed Kroger. Bess watched as Devereaux received accolades of gratitude with just the right note of pleased modesty. The major saw Fargo, detached himself from the crowd, and walked over with Bess at his side.

"Willing to admit you were wrong, Fargo?" Devereaux said. "No reneging this time. He kept his bargain. He saw I meant business."

"He never figured to do anything else," Fargo said. "He got what he wanted, his brother the first time, the rifles the second."

"He'll have his campfire stories to tell. I've the people back. It's finished," Devereaux said smugly.

"Hell it is. He's got you up shit creek. You can't even send out regular patrols, not with the firepower he has now," Fargo said.

"I'll send out double-strength patrols," the major said.

"You can't do that without leaving the compound undermanned and he knows it. He'll have scouts watching, but he'll be able to move free and easy without even thinking about you. This isn't an end. It's a beginning," Fargo said.

Devereaux offered one of his tolerantly patient smiles. "Stay around, Fargo. You'll be eating those words," he said. "You've got to learn to admit when you've been wrong." He walked away on sure, confident steps and Fargo brought his eyes to Bess as she studied him thoughtfully.

"There's being stubborn and there's being obstinate, you know," she said reprovingly.

"And there's being blind," he snapped. The honey-wheat hair sent off flashes of gold as she whirled and strode into the compound.

"Let's get a drink," Fargo heard Titus say, and he nodded agreement.

"You notice anything when Red Claw had his braves all lined up?" Fargo asked on the way to the saloon.

"Same thing you noticed. Nokato wasn't there," the old guide said. "You know what that means."

"Yep." Fargo nodded. "He's being kept in camp as punishment for letting himself be taken by the troopers. It's common custom with many tribes. A man's disciplined for his mistakes or stupidity."

"Seeing as how much trouble he's caused, I'd guess he's drawn at least a couple of weeks discipline," Titus said. "What's buzzing around your mind, young feller? You're not just interested in Arapaho tribal discipline."

Fargo frowned as they halted before the saloon. "Nothing that's got any shape yet," Fargo said. "Let's get that drink and hope it's not the last one." Titus followed him into the dance hall, where it was plain that business had returned to normal, the bar crowded, most of the tables filled, an atmosphere of gaiety as thick as the smoke in the air. Fargo ordered bourbons and downed his quickly. Titus finished but half of his when he turned, his lined face crinkling into a parchment grimace.

"I can't stand all this celebrating. Let's get out of here," he said, and followed Fargo from the saloon. Outside, the day had slid into afternoon as they rode from town and finally halted on a hill that faced Shadow Mountain. "Think he'll settle back?" Titus asked as he peered at the purplish distance and the great mountain that rose majestically into the sky.

"Would you?" Fargo grunted, and Titus spat to his right. "A cougar sees a weak antelope he stays after it," Fargo added.

Titus turned to survey the terrain in the other direction with a long, slow sweep. "There's no saying how a wagon train will travel," he said. "But I'd guess that valley down there and the narrow plateau to the east would attract most."

"Come morning, you take the valley and I'll take the plateau. Most we can do is try to warn them to turn back," Fargo said. "It'll be an off chance but we can try."

Titus nodded in silence and followed Fargo as the

big man turned the Ovaro down into a grassy knoll where the hackberry grew thick. A shaded thicket beckoned and Fargo pulled into the spot and slid from the saddle as the day began to wane. "Good a spot as any to bed down," he said. "We can go both ways easily from here come morning." He brought out some strips of beef jerky and ate with the old guide as darkness descended and he finally stretched out in inky blackness. A wind came up to rustle the trees and he felt the grim smile touch his lips. It was but a harbinger of the storm that was yet to explode.

6

The morning sun had grown hot as Fargo rode the long, narrow plateau and halted at a trickling stream to let the Ovaro drink. He'd seen no fresh wagon wheel tracks but he had seen new, unshod Indian pony tracks, a single rider moving southward across the plateau. A lone scout, Fargo grunted grimly. But there were more, he knew, moving like wraiths through the hills and valleys. When the horse finished drinking, he turned north to seek out Titus when he glimpsed the thin spiral of trail dust to the east in the direction of Owlshead.

He changed course, put the pinto into a canter, and moved over the low slopes and inclines, through a stand of black oak. As he rode, his eyes stayed on the thin line of dust as it moved westward. Disciplined riders in a close group, he saw, keeping a steady pace. Though the line of dust stayed thin, it was more than unshod Indian ponies would have raised on the fresh, moist terrain, and when he topped a rise, the column of blue-uniformed horsemen didn't surprise him. Some twenty troopers, he estimated, but he felt the sharp intake of his breath when he saw the honey-wheat hair glistening in the sunlight.

From beneath his lowered, frowning brows, he saw Devereaux riding beside Bess, both a dozen yards ahead of the column of troopers. The major brought the column to a halt as Fargo rode up, a patiently anticipatory half smile on the older man's face. "What the hell is she doing out here?" Fargo growled.

"Obviously taking a ride with me," Devereaux said with bemused calm.

"I was growing stir-crazy sitting around the compound," Bess added.

Fargo's eyes stayed on the major. "What are you trying to do?" he pressed.

"You said Red Claw would have scouts out watching and I quite agree that he will," Devereaux said. "I want him to see that we're sending out patrols as usual. Lieutenant Baker has a column of forty troopers patrolling northwest There are a number of settlements throughout the entire north territory that come under my protection."

"Still doesn't explain her," Fargo said.

"It's important that Red Claw see that we're not the least bit intimidated by the fact that he has rifles. His scouts will tell him that I'm so unconcerned that I took my daughter out with me," Devereaux said.

"Only one thing wrong," Fargo said. "This isn't going to impress him one damn bit."

"What makes you say that?" Devereaux frowned as he bristled.

"Because you can't impress him, Major. He knows you now. It's too late for this kind of grandstand play," Fargo said.

Anger wiped the amused tolerance from the man's face. "You insist on overestimating him and underestimating me, Fargo," he barked.

"Jesus, I wish you were right," Fargo bit out, and caught Bess's glare. He started to turn the pinto just as the rider appeared over the top of the nearest slope, riding hard, spindly long legs flapping against the side of the brown mare. Fargo waited as Titus reined to a hard halt, his leathered face wrinkled in disgust.

"Come looking to find you," Titus said to the big man. "Lower end of valley, three wagons burned, everybody taken off."

It was Bess who gave voice to the words that ran through everyone else. "He's taken more hostages," she gasped out.

"Damn his savage soul," Devereaux rasped, and threw a sharp glance at Titus. "Any point in our going into the valley?" he asked.

"Not unless you like lookin' at burned wagons," Titus returned.

"Let's get back to town," Devereaux said, waved an arm at the column of blue to his rear, and set off at a fast trot. Fargo and Titus swung in behind Bess and her father as they rode back toward Owlshead. The stockade fence of the compound came in sight and Bess peeled off as the major led the column through the gate. Titus rode slowly on into town as Bess Devereaux brought her horse around to Fargo's side and Fargo saw the frown furrow her smooth brow, her gray-blue eyes peering at him.

"You keep on being right, Fargo," she said thoughtfully.

"You keep being surprised," he remarked.

"I guess so," Bess said soberly.

"That bothers you," he said, and her lips tightened even as she nodded. "Makes it harder to look away each time," he added.

The gray-blue eyes took on instant protectiveness. "Being wrong isn't being weak," she said.

"They can go together," he said quietly, and she turned her face away for a moment. He took in the loveliness of her, the honey-wheat hair falling alongside the fine line of her jaw, lips that could be sensuously full, the straight line of her nose, a face delicate yet strong. She returned her eyes to him, deep caring in their depths.

"What can he demand now?" she asked.

"The moon, the sky, whatever he wants." Fargo shrugged.

"My father won't keep giving in," Bess said.

"He suddenly going to get a backbone?" Fargo flared.

"That's rotten," she flung back.

"It's true," he said. "How's it going to look on a report when he sacrifices some hostages and not others?"

"I don't know," she said angrily.

"He wasn't strong enough to say no twice. He won't be strong enough to say it now," Fargo told her. "And I'm sorry, for you, for everybody."

"He'll find a way," Bess Devereaux said, but there was as much hope as loyalty in her voice. She started to move away and halted. "Can you help?" she asked, her eyes peering deep into his.

"I don't know," he said. "Maybe it's too late." She took his answer in for a long moment and slowly, silently, rode into the compound. "Shit," he muttered to himself as he sent the Ovaro on down the main street of town. He looked for the deep-chested brown mare outside the saloon but the horse wasn't there and he rode on. He passed the old granary and went out of town, heading straight along the road until he finally spied Titus atop a low hill about a mile beyond town. Fargo rode up to where the old guide looked across the land that seemed only peaceful and lush with greenery.

"Been trying to figure a way to get at that Arapaho," Titus said. "Haven't come up with anything, though."

"I thought about it while I was riding this morning," Fargo said. "Didn't do any better. Might not be a way. He's got all the cards now."

"We'll be finding out what his next move is all too soon," Titus said. "We won't be happy about it, that's for sure."

Fargo nodded grimly and moved the pinto forward down the slope as Titus followed alongside. He rode across a wide swatch of ground thick with pigeon grass and shot a quick glance at Titus as he suddenly heard the sound of galloping hooves. He watched the incline directly ahead as the sound grew louder, the rattle of rein chains now clear along with the hoofbeats. In minutes, the double column of troopers came into sight, Lieutenant Baker in the lead. The young officer brought his platoon to a halt and Fargo saw the tight line around his mouth.

"Arapaho, about two miles back. They ambushed us, jumped us from both sides in a short passway between two stands of black oak," the lieutenant said between deep drafts of breath. "Some fifty of them, I'd guess. They had us between them and outgunned. I figured running was the best thing we could do. We lost six men."

"You did right, son," Titus said. "You'd have lost a lot more if you'd tried to stop and fight in an ambush."

"The major will say I should've circled when I got out of the passway and come back at them," the lieutenant said glumly.

"With them all waiting and ready for you?" Titus snapped. "You tell the major I said you did right."

Fargo smiled at the expression of dubiousness that Baker was unable to keep from his face.

"Maybe he'll send out a small burial party in the morning," the lieutenant said.

"Thanks for warning us," Fargo said as Baker waved his platoon forward.

"Going to have a look?" Titus asked as the troopers receded toward Owlshead, and Fargo nodded.

"A war party that size won't hang around long," he said, but he moved forward carefully, his gaze sweeping the terrain on all sides as he rode. He slowed when he came in sight of the two stands of black oaks, nosed in between the trees with caution.

"Over there, on the right," Titus said from a few paces behind him, and Fargo steered the horse to where the six bodies had been pulled to one side. All were stripped naked and Fargo felt the frown dig into his brow. "Bastards," Titus spit out. The practice was not uncommon, especially among some tribes, but it was not an Arapaho characteristic. It was perhaps one more message of contempt on Red Claw's part, Fargo pondered, and pointed to the pony tracks. "They took their loot and left," Titus said. "Didn't try to chase after the platoon at all."

"Maybe they had orders not to get into heavy fighting," Fargo said. "Let's head back." He turned the pinto and, Titus at his heels, set off at a canter as the purple gray of twilight began to filter across the land. The night descended when he rode into Owlshead and halted at the general store where Molly and Ed Kroger put groceries into a yellow pony wagon.

"I'll be at Dolly's," Titus said, and rode on.

Fargo saw the worry in Ed Kroger's eyes as the man stepped toward him. "Word is all over about the new hostages," Kroger said. "Guess you were right about it not stopping."

"Guess so," Fargo remarked blandly.

"Folks are worried, wondering what it means for us. A committee went to ask the major about it," Kroger said.

"What'd he tell them?" Fargo asked.

"That it wouldn't likely affect us. It'd be over the new hostages and he'd deal with that," Kroger said.

Fargo swung down from the horse and felt the anger inside himself. "The major's a goddamn horse's ass," he bit out. "There's nothing going to happen that won't bear on all of you." He turned and strode away, leading the pinto behind him. He hadn't gone half the street when she stepped out of the shadows, a swirl of honey-wheat hair.

"You have to talk like that about my father?" Bess Devereaux challenged with ice on each word.

"He lied to those people," Fargo said.

"You don't know that. Maybe he believed what he told them," she countered.

"Then he's just what I said he was," Fargo threw at her. Bess Devereaux's lips opened, closed tight as she turned her face away from him. "You taken up eavesdropping?" he asked harshly.

"No," she said. "I was actually looking for you. I came near when I saw you stop. I couldn't help overhear."

"What put you to looking for me?" he asked, and halted in the deep shadows of an overhang in front of the town barber shop.

"I came looking to tell you I'm sorry about the way it always ends up," she told him.

"How's that?"

"With our fighting over the things you say," she answered. "You saved my life. I wanted to tell you I haven't forgotten that. I'm very afraid, suddenly, and I wanted you to know that before anything else happens." She paused and a wry smile touched her fine-lined lips. "Confession's good for the soul, I've been told," she said.

"Words are easy," Fargo said.

She frowned in thought for a moment. "Yes, I suppose so," she said, and suddenly her arms were around his neck, her lips pressed upon his, warm, sweet tasting, moving against his with soft insistence, her breasts full and deep against his chest. "Proof enough?" she asked as she pulled back.

"Yes." He nodded and his hand tightened around the long, slender waist, drew her to him again, and her lips opened at his kiss and he tasted the quick, soft point of her tongue before she pulled back again. "I could find a place," he murmured.

"No," she breathed. "I won't do any more saying now, with words or without them. There's too much unfinished yet for more."

"Maybe," he said, and smiled at the flicker of reluctant self-control in her eyes as she stepped back. But she knew he understood and he let her walk on with quick steps, as though she feared she might change her mind. She disappeared into the darkness as she hurried to the compound and he slowly walked to the dance hall, tethered the Ovaro outside, and went into the noisy, smoke-filled room. He found Titus waiting for him at a table with a bourbon ready and he slid into the chair.

"Took you a spell," Titus remarked.

"Met up with Bess Devereaux," Fargo said.

"She still looking for answers?" Titus asked.

"She understands, more than she wants to," Fargo said as he drew on the bourbon and felt the liquid curl inside him. He had another and some of the ham and eggs Titus had ordered and watched the crowd as the

93

evening wore on. "How about we sleep in real beds tonight, old man?" he asked Titus. "My treat."

"Won't catch me turning down an offer like that," Titus said, and Fargo beckoned Dolly to the table.

"You got two extra rooms for the night?" he asked.

"For you and Titus? Anytime," the woman said, and let her eyes move over the big man's chiseled handsomeness. "Just rooms?" she asked.

"Just rooms." Fargo laughed. "Want peace, quiet, and thinking time."

"Whatever you say. Let me know if you change your mind. You stayed around when you could've rode out. That deserves something," Dolly said.

"Fair enough," Fargo said, and slowly finished his bourbon as Dolly returned to moving among the tables. Later, the bartender brought two room keys to the table and Fargo tossed one to Titus as he rose to his feet. "I'm going to make the most of a night in a real bed," he said. "See you in the morning, old-timer."

"I'll be turning in soon, too," Titus said, and Fargo made his way through the crowd to a back stairway and climbed to the second floor. He found the room at the end of a short corridor, opened the door, and took in a plain, small room with a single bed and battered dresser. But it was neat and swept clean and he undressed, put his holster across the top of the bedpost. Naked, he slid under the sheet and stretched out. He reached over to the single kerosene lamp and turned it off and the darkness wrapped itself around him at once. He lay awake, letting thoughts tumble through his mind in unconnected sequence, quietly hoping for some subconscious flintstone to strike sparks that would offer a plan, a thought, a hope. But the thoughts remained draped in grimness and he finally shut out their depressing parade and closed his eyes.

He was almost asleep when he heard the faint knock

at the door and he sat up, drew the Colt from its holster, and turned the lamp on low. "Come in," he called. "It's open." He watched the doorknob slowly turn and he lowered the Colt as the girl stepped almost shyly into the room, smallish, outfitted in a bare-shouldered green dress. He took in brown hair, a young, pretty enough face under too much powder and paint, an eighteen-year-old's figure, still a little gangly but slender and attractive.

"Hello," she said, and closed the door behind her. "I'm Clara. Dolly sent me up. She said it was on the house."

"Dolly's a warmhearted woman." Fargo laughed and put the Colt away. He surveyed the girl again and caught the shadow of shyness once more. "You're new, I'll bet," he said.

"Just started tonight. Dolly said you'd like that, being first and all," she answered.

"First here, you mean." He laughed and she gave a tiny shrug and her eyes took on a glimmer of worldliness beyond her years. "What the hell," Fargo murmured. Losing himself with a pair of warm and willing legs, even if they weren't the ones he'd have chosen, might make the world seem a better place. "Come on over here, Clara," he said, and drew a quick, happy smile. She reached one hand behind her, undid a clasp, and the top of the dress fell open and he took in nice, round breasts, on the small side but fitting the rest of her. She wriggled and the dress fell to the floor and he saw narrow hips, a young girl's figure unquestionably, with a small, black triangle and below it, legs with just enough curve in them not to be skinny. She moved on quick, bouncy steps and fell onto the bed alongside him and her breasts came against his chest. The sheet fell away and he saw her eyes grow appreciative as she took in the powerful, muscled beauty that was his and the already expanding, rising organ.

"Jeez," she breathed, and brought one leg up across his hips, rolled, then pressed her small nap down over his maleness and rubbed back and forth. She leaned forward and he cupped one small breast in his hand, let his thumb move over the little, flat nipple that continued to stay flat. But his maleness had popped free to stand tall and throbbing and the warm tip pressed against the girl's soft portal. "Oh, Jeez," Clara breathed. She wriggled her small rear, pushed it backward and brought herself down onto him. "Ah, ah . . . aaaaah," she gasped out as she sank over him.

It has happening too fast but it continued to explode in quick, sensual explosion as Clara pumped her slender hips up and down atop him, plunging deep over him, lifting plunging down again and she brought the small breasts up to his mouth, pushed down over his lips with one. He sucked, caressed, and she continued to pump and sat up for greater leverage, and he saw the enjoyment on her young face. Clara was not hurrying out of duty but exploding with a sweep of pleasure that was beyond acting.

"Ah, ah, ah, Jeez . . . Jeez, ah, ah," she gasped out with each plunge, and he lifted his hips, thrust upward and brought her with him and she half screamed. Suddenly Clara's young face pulled up, her head straining backward and little veins in her neck bulging. "Oh, Jeez, I'm coming . . . oh, Christ, now, now . . . iiieeeeee," Clara screamed, and there was as much surprise as ecstasy in her voice and he let himself go with her and she felt the throbbing of him and screamed with renewed pleasure.

She kept pumping until, like a balloon suddenly deflated, she collapsed over him and lay panting atop him, still holding him inside her. "Jeez," she breathed, "oh, Jeez." Slowly her legs grew straight and she let herself slide from him with another shuddered breath.

"You don't waste any damn time, do you, honey?" Fargo said.

Her eyes were round as she stared at him. "It never happened like this before to me," she said with a sense of awe in her voice. "I looked at you and Jesus, it all came over me like a wave."

"Maybe it was a combination of things," Fargo said. "It was good, that's what counts."

"Oh, Jeez, yes," the girl said, and rolled against him. "But I'd like another go at it, slower this time."

"Good idea," Fargo said, and held her against him as she lay still, gathering in deep breaths, her slender body wrapped around him. When she lifted her face to him, he saw her lips open, reaching upward, and he brought his mouth to hers. Her lips pressed hard and he felt her tongue come at once, darting forward, smooth, sliding messenger of the senses. He had just cupped his hand around one small breast when the first fusillade of gunfire erupted outside. Another followed, and then a steady explosion of rifle fire and the sound of galloping hooves. The wild war whoops followed and he heard the charge of horses down the street outside the window.

He swung out of bed and the girl hit the floor as he leaped over her to peer out the window where he saw a half-dozen Arapahos racing down the street, shooting wildly. He felt the frown digging hard into his brow as he flew into clothes and raced from the room still strapping his gunbelt on. He met Titus in the hallway as the old guide charged from his room and followed him downstairs. Much of the bar had cleared and Fargo dropped to one knee as he pushed through the doors to the street and a hail of bullets smashed into the side of the building. Four Arapahos raced by firing and Fargo took aim at the last one that went by, fired, and the Indian toppled sideways from his horse to lie still in the center of main street.

The heavy thunder of rifle fire resounded from the end of town and Fargo heard Titus come alongside him. "They're attacking the compound," the old guide said, the surprise stark in his voice.

"Goddamn, that doesn't fit. The Arapaho don't attack by night," Fargo said.

"No, but they're doin' it, by God," Titus said, and rose as Fargo darted for the Ovaro.

"Let's go see," Fargo said, and vaulted into the saddle, cast a glance behind him as he raced down main street. There were no other charging red-skinned horsemen coming up the street and he galloped the Ovaro toward the north end of Owlshead where the war whoops and the heavy thunder of rifle fire still filled the air. He slowed as he neared the compound and saw the Arapahos racing back and forth at the front of the stockade fence, firing wildly and staying almost out of range. A line of troopers returned fire from the top of the stockade fence and Fargo bent low in the saddle as a half-dozen attackers raced toward the far end of the compound and instantly drew fire from another set of defenders. Fargo glanced back into town and saw only empty streets. The Arapahos had made a few charging passes through town but their main force attacked the compound and the frown on Fargo's face deepened.

It was a strange attack, not only because it came by night but because it seemed mostly wild shooting and furious back-and-forth charges nearly out of range. From the heads atop the stockade, it appeared Devereaux had his entire force manning the stockade wall facing the defenders. "Stay here and watch your head," Fargo muttered to Titus. "I'm going to circle around to the back of the compound." He wheeled the pinto in a tight maneuver and, still staying low in the saddle, sent the horse around the rear corner of the compound. He reined to a halt as he glimpsed three blue-coated figures racing into the darkness, their backs to him, and as he watched in astonishment, two more blue-uniformed figures came over the rear wall of the stockade, lowering themselves with catlike speed on two ropes.

As the first one dropped to the ground, his cap came off and Fargo saw the long, black hair cascade into sight. "Son-of-a-bitch," he swore as he sent the Ovaro racing forward. He brought the Colt up as the figure spun, saw him coming, and tried to run. Fargo's shot split the man's head open and the figure seemed to come apart as it jerked and wobbled convulsively before it hit the ground. Fargo glimpsed the other blue-uniformed figure whirl and toss the tomahawk, a viciously quick and accurate throw. Fargo had only time to dive sideways out of the saddle as the weapon grazed his head. He hit the ground on all fours and felt the jar of it go through his shoulders, the Colt falling from his grasp. He glanced up to see the figure diving for the gun and he flung a sideways blow with one arm that hit the man across the shoulders, only enough force behind it to make him miss getting hold of the gun.

His uniform hat fell off and once again Fargo saw the thick, stringy black hair that had been hidden under the cap. The Arapaho yanked a knife from inside his belt and brought his arm back as he dived with a snarl of fury. Fargo held his position on one knee for as long as he dared before flinging himself sideways, his legs hitting the Arapaho in the chest as the Indian dived past. Fargo landed on the ground, whirled, and saw the brave pushing himself to his feet for another charge. Fargo rolled, came up on his feet as the Arapaho lunged, swiped viciously with the knife, and Fargo avoided the blow by a fraction of an inch as he leaped backward.

The lunge brought the man off-balance, and before he could turn, Fargo's right fist came around to crash onto the back of his foe's neck. The hammerlike blow drove the Arapaho forward and down on one knee and Fargo brought a whistling left hook around that caught the man on the point of the jaw. The Indian left the ground as he flew backward, landed on his back, and rolled, but he kept hold of the knife. Fargo made a quick lunging dive for the Colt still on the ground. He got his hand around the butt of the gun as the Arapaho charged again, the knife upraised. Fargo barely managed to bring the gun up in time to fire and he saw the bullet slam into the charging figure at the base of his neck. Suddenly gushing red, the Indian stumbled forward and Fargo rolled out of the way, turned, and saw the man fall facedown. He was still making guttural, garbled sounds while he twitched and Fargo pushed to his feet.

The sounds stopped as Fargo went to the stockade wall and took hold of one of the ropes and saw it was a long length of rawhide knotted with other lengths to form a thin but very strong rope. As he took hold of the end and began to pull himself up on the stockade fence, he realized the rifle fire had halted and he heard the sound of the Arapahos racing into the night. He reached the top of the stockade rear wall and swung over onto the platform that ran the length of it a few feet below. He saw the still forms of two troopers lying facedown on the platform.

He looked across at the front wall where the defenders had stopped firing. Among the troopers he spotted a dozen of the settlers whose families stayed inside the cabins within the compound. Fargo started to climb down the wooden steps that led to the top of the rear wall and saw Devereaux turning away from the front of the compound.

The major saw him and frowned. "How'd you get in here?" he asked.

"Over the rear wall, the way they did," Fargo said.

"They?" the major questioned.

"At least five of them. I got two as they reached the ground outside. They were wearing troopers uniforms, all of them," Fargo said. The frown on his brow stayed and he felt the bitter taste in his mouth as the pieces began to fall into place. "That attack was just a damn diversion. So were those passes they made through town. It was planned to get you concentrating fire and attention on the front wall while they sneaked a half-dozen men in over the back," Fargo said. "That explains the six troopers they stripped. They wanted their uniforms. You and your men weren't going to notice a few more troopers running through the compound."

"My God," Devereaux breathed. "Why? What'd they do in here?"

Fargo shrugged. "I don't know. The two I got were empty-handed but I did catch sight of the others running away. Couldn't really see anything, though."

Devereaux spun and barked orders at a nearby sergeant. "Take a dozen men. Search the compound," he said.

"What are we looking for, sir?" the sergeant asked.

"I don't know, dammit," Devereaux shouted. "Just tell me anything you find out of place. Maybe they made off with more ammunition or more rifles." He glanced at Fargo as the sergeant hurried away. "You come with me. I want to talk about tomorrow. I'll be getting a new set of demands, I'm certain." Fargo followed the man into his quarters where the lamps were on in the front room and in the adjoining room. "Bess, come here a moment, please," Devereaux called.

Fargo followed his gaze to the open door of the next room. "She stay inside when the shooting started?" Fargo asked.

"I told her to," the major said. "Bess, you in there?" he called, and again received no answer. He strode to the doorway and Fargo fell in behind him as an icy hand suddenly tore at his innards. Devereaux pushed the door open and Fargo hissed the single word. "Shit," he said, his glance taking in the chairs knocked over, the torn piece of blouse hanging from the bedpost.

"Oh, my God," Devereaux breathed. "Oh, my God." Fargo met the ashen, horror-stricken face that turned to him and he could stare back only with bitterness.

"Your early morning ride with her sure impressed him," Fargo said, and saw Devereaux slump down into a chair, a man drained of everything but horror. Fargo turned and walked from the room, crossed to the front door and flung it open, and strode into the night. Inside him, the seething, helpless rage churned. All the pieces fit perfectly now. The Arapaho chief had seen his chance, gone into action with every step planned. Devereaux deserved every bit of the tearing, ripping pain that slashed at him, Fargo cursed. He was reaping the rewards an arrogant, stupid, weak man deserved. And as it always happened, others would pay the price and he thought of the honey-wheat hair and the delicate yet strong face. She'd need all that inner strength that was hers, he snorted in silent anger. The troopers had opened the front gate of the compound again and he saw Titus enter leading the Ovaro. The old guide's face seemed to have taken on a few more creases as he stared at the big man.

"Saw the two by the wall out back. I've already put

some of the pieces together. What's the rest of it?" Titus asked.

"Red Claw has seen to it that the major won't be saying no to anything he demands," Fargo said, and saw Titus blink his eyes closed for a second.

"That bastard. The stinking, rotten, murdering bastard," Titus muttered. "Where's Devereaux?"

"In his quarters, coming apart," Fargo grunted. "We'll bed down here for the rest of the night. There's not a lot of it left." Titus nodded and drew the horses over to a corner of the compound where the shadows were deep. Lieutenant Baker had taken charge, Fargo saw, posted six sentries on each wall, dispatched the rest of the men to their barracks. As he watched, he saw the sergeant report back to Baker.

"Didn't find anything out of order anywhere, sir," he heard the sergeant say, and the lieutenant started for Devereaux's quarters.

"Hold on, Lieutenant," Fargo said, and stepped forward. "No need to report to the major." Baker halted, frowned at him. "They took Bess," Fargo added, and the young officer's jaw dropped open.

"Good God," Baker gasped. "Good God." He stared, transfixed for a moment, and suddenly pulled himself back. "Why didn't you tell me before this? We could've gone after them!"

"There's no way in hell you'd catch them," Fargo said. "All you'd do is get more of your men killed. You'll have enough chance at that before this is over."

He turned from the soldier and strode back to the corner where the deep shadows shut out the rest of the compound. He stretched out on his bedroll and wondered which was worse, a foe that was as cunning as he was ruthless or an ally as stupid as he was weak. He went to sleep with a curse still hanging on his lips.

Using the inner clock he'd long ago learned to set,

he woke with the first dawn, dressed hurriedly, and washed at a nearby water keg. He saw Titus struggle awake as he hurried into the major's quarters. Devereaux was dressed, his uniform crisp, his face a haggard mask. Fargo heard the sentry's shout of alarm from outside and the major rose to his feet.

"He's come," Fargo said.

"Just you," Devereaux said. "I won't dignify him by a show of force."

"You won't fool him, either," Fargo grunted, and left the building with the officer. Fargo swung onto the Ovaro and rode out beside Devereaux to see Red Claw alone on the white pony. The major put his mount into a gallop and reined to a sharp halt in front of the Arapaho chief.

"You stinking, rotten bastard," Devereaux spat out. "Where's my daughter, damn you? Where is she?" He glared at Fargo. "Tell him what I just said," the major ordered.

"Some things don't need translating," Fargo answered, and waited as Devereaux glared at the Indian's stone face. He moved the Ovaro to face Red Claw directly. "Speak," he said.

The Indian's black-coal eyes flickered and he shot out words in short clusters and, inside himself, Fargo felt a combination of rage and reluctant admiration for the Arapaho chief. Perhaps the ultimate, bitter irony of it was lost on him, Fargo mused. He didn't know the ways of the white man's conscience but he knew how to break the weak. He knew it too damn well, Fargo swore, and turned to Devereaux.

"What's he after this time?" the major asked, his arrogance quick to return.

"You're to move the regiment out, lock, stock, and barrel, close up shop, and ride south," Fargo said.

"He can't mean that," Devereaux gasped.

"He means every damn word of it. You leave with the regiment or Bess and the other hostages he has will be killed," Fargo said.

"Tell him I can't just ride off," Devereaux protested.

"Don't waste time being a fool," Fargo snapped. "He knows you can ride out just the way you rode in."

"Buy some time, dammit," Devereaux said, and Fargo turned back to the Indian chief. The stone face hadn't changed expression but Fargo thought he detected a spark of smug confidence in the black-coal eyes.

"We will talk again," he said.

"Tomorrow," Red Claw answered. "You answer tomorrow." Fargo watched the Arapaho turn his pony and calmly disappear into the trees.

"He won't get away with it, damn his soul," Devereaux muttered. "I'm going to take the entire regiment on a full-scale attack on his camp. That's the only way to save Bess. Go in and take her."

"She won't be there," Fargo said. "He expects you might try that. He won't have her there. She's hidden away someplace by now."

Fargo watched the angry bravado disappear in Devereaux's eyes, replaced by the hollow stare of the broken and defeated. The man wheeled his mount and rode back to the compound at a gallop. He pushed through the crowd that had gathered, dismounted, and strode into his quarters and Fargo saw the faces turn to him as he rode up. In each face he saw apprehension, fear, uncertainty and he spoke quickly, told them exactly what Red Claw had set out as his price for Bess Devereaux and the others. He heard the gasp of dismay that rose from the crowd.

"What's the major going to do?" Ed Kroger called out, one arm around his wife.

"He didn't tell me. Ask him yourself when you've a mind," Fargo said, and turned away. The crowd began to break up into small knots of figures. They'd talk, exchange their fears, and come back later for answers, he was certain, and he strode to where Titus waited.

"I'd say we're between a rock and a hard place with nowhere to go," Titus observed. "That damn Indian holds all the cards now for sure."

"He's sure he's won everything he wants. Maybe we can turn that around on him," Fargo said, and saw Titus frown back. "Got to think some more," Fargo said, and led the pinto with him as he walked from the compound. He went only far enough to find a good shade tree where he settled down, his back against the trunk, and closed his eyes. But this time he disciplined the thoughts that tried to race through his mind, forced them into patterns and ordered sequences. Finally, when each mental excursion led to the same place, he rose, his eyes narrowed in thought as he started back to the compound. He had a plan, such as it was, a thing of fragile connections and desperate pieces. But it was the only one, he was convinced of that, and he quickened his pace toward the compound as he saw the crowd gathering outside the major's quarters.

He elbowed his way in, moved to one side near the building, and saw Molly standing with Emily and Ed Kroger. She caught his glance and he thought he caught a flash of apology in her eyes. The major came from his office with Lieutenant Baker at his side and Fargo saw the arrogance gone from the man, replaced by fear and desperation. "We come to hear what you're going to do about that Indian's demands, Major," a man called out.

"Do? There's only one thing I can do to save the lives of the hostages he's holding. Do what he wants. Take the regiment and pull out," Devereaux said.

"You can't do that. It'll leave us all without protection," the man said.

"Not just us," a woman put in. "All the folks in the northwest, in Claresville, Otter Junction, up in Juniper. I've cousins settled just outside Fork Hills. We'll all be massacred once he has the whole territory to himself."

"I'll come back, soon as I know the hostages are all safe," Devereaux said.

"He won't let you. He'll figure out a way to keep you away," another woman said.

"Fargo was right the first time. I can see that now," Ed Kroger said. "It only gets worse."

Fargo made a wry sound. "It's easy to see the light on somebody else's back," he snorted.

"Dammit, you all have your families back," Devereaux said. "He has my daughter. I gave in to him for you. I can't do less for her. I'm pulling out come morning. You'd all better start making plans to protect yourselves. The compound's yours. It can hold everybody in town." He turned and strode into his quarters and Fargo watched the uncomfortableness in the faces that turned to each other. Slowly, the crowd began to drift away in small knots of sober-faced people.

"He put it to them, I'll give him credit for that," Fargo heard Titus say at his elbow.

"Almost the truth," Fargo said, and Titus questioned with a glance. "He made his giving in sound like a noble gesture. He gave in because he was too weak to do what was right, too concerned about how it'd look in a report to Washington. No guts, no nobility."

Titus gave a grim snort. "You hang hard, don't you, young feller?" he said.

"Anything else puts a man down the wrong trail,"

Fargo said, and Titus went with him as he strode into the major's quarters.

Devereaux looked up and Fargo saw the half-empty shot glass on the desk. "The gall of them, asking me to turn my back on my own daughter," the man spat out, his eyes hollow with dark and churning emotions, bitter defensiveness in the forefront. "And you, you still stick to that stand of yours, no trading for hostages, now that it's Bess he's got?" Devereaux flung out.

Fargo felt the bitterness of his words well up inside him. "Yes," he murmured, and hated the saying of it. "But that's no matter now. It's too late for talk, too late for anything but action. You've got to get back the only ace card you ever held."

"Nokato," Titus grunted.

"He's our one chance. We'll never find where Bess has been hidden but we know where Nokato is," Fargo said.

"Begging your pardon, sir," the voice cut in, and he turned to see the lieutenant in the doorway. "I couldn't help overhearing and we could never fight through the Arapaho to seize Nokato. They outman us and, with those rifles, outgun us."

"I know that," Fargo said. "But we're going to give Red Claw some of his own medicine back. We're going to make a diversionary raid, make it look like the real thing, just as he did here. He's too cocky now to expect that. He's half expecting a raid to free Bess, anyway. He'll turn out everyone except for Nokato and a few others. Nokato's still being disciplined. Take fifty men, leave the rest here with the major."

"Now just a moment," Devereaux bristled. "I'm heading the command around here. I don't take orders from civilians."

Fargo paused, swallowed the words that came to his

tongue. It wasn't time to spear the man through, not yet. "This is only the first step. The important part comes later. I want you unhurt, ready to lead that part of it," Fargo said. "There's no time to go into the details now but I've worked it all out carefully."

"When will you be back?" Devereaux asked, the question an acceptance.

"Before morning if it goes right," Fargo said, turned on his heel, and strode from the room. He waited outside for Baker to follow and walked to the stables with him. "We'll talk more on the way. Meanwhile, you pick out four of your best men for me," he said, and the lieutenant nodded as he hurried to get the squad turned out.

The sun was in the noon sky when Fargo rode from the compound, Titus beside him, the lieutenant and his troopers following. "Straight on to Shadow Mountain," Fargo said. "It'll be dark when we get there." He put the Ovaro into a ground-eating trot and rested only twice to let the horses drink and soon the purple-gray bulk of Shadow Mountain loomed up in front of him as the night descended. He halted, drew in a deep breath and smelt the odor of wood burning. "Their camp's straight ahead." He turned to Baker. "They'll know you're coming before you reach them," he said. "Where are the four men I want?"

The lieutenant motioned and four troopers detached themselves from the others and came up. Fargo saw four men with some years on them, each steady-eyed with no uneasiness in their faces. "You four come with me," he said. "When you charge in, Lieutenant, do plenty of shooting but don't try to make a fight of it. When they really come at you, fall back, get out of the trees, and draw them after you. Run for it and let them chase you. They'll give up soon." The lieutenant nodded and Fargo motioned to the four troopers.

"Give us fifteen minutes head start," he said, and with Titus behind him set off in a wide circle through the trees.

The odor of the woodfires grew stronger as Fargo circled around to the rear of the camp and little flickering flares of orange light penetrated the dark of the thick woodland. Fargo halted, his voice hardly audible. "Take the bits out of your horses' mouths, tie the rein chains, fold your stirrups over the saddle. Put any loose change in your pockets into your kerchiefs, same for watches, pens, anything that could rattle." He waited while the men followed his orders and then started forward again. "I'll take Nokato but I want four others alive. I don't care if they're men or women. Knock them out and sling them on your horses," he said.

"An eye for an eye?" Titus commented.

"Red Claw's going to get real rough after this. That's the only thing he'll understand," Fargo said.

"You're right but that doesn't make it any less nasty," Titus said.

"It doesn't," Fargo agreed, and fell silent as the Arapaho camp came into sight. A full-scale camp, he saw, with at least four tepees, plenty of squaws and kids. A meat-drying rack stood at one end and Fargo's eyes slowly traveled across the camp as he moved closer to the back side of it. About seventy-five warriors, he guessed, most of the braves stretched out along the far side of the camp. He'd demanded a hundred and fifty rifles, Fargo mused. He planned to arm and recruit other Arapaho tribes when he began his rampage across the territory.

Fargo dropped to one knee in the trees and motioned for the troopers to stretch out in a line alongside the camp. Again, his gaze moved across the camp until it finally came to a halt on the three figures seated near one of the tepees. On Nokato's bony face was the sneer he remembered from when Devereaux had set him free. The other two looked merely sullen. Fargo had just started to wonder about the lieutenant when he saw a brave race into the camp, shouting excitedly and followed by another. The flap of the largest tepee flew open instantly and Red Claw emerged, barking commands, and Fargo watched the nearly naked bronze forms galvanize into action, leaping onto their barebacked ponies. Red Claw appeared again through the melee, on the white pony this time, and Fargo watched him lead the charge into the forest. The thunder of rifle fire exploded in the night, all but drowning out the shouts and war whoops. The lieutenant was laying down a heavy barrage, Fargo noted in satisfaction, and he watched Nokato and the other two braves stand and peer into the forest, their backs to him. He took another quick sweep of the camp. Six or so old men were nearby, as were a handful of squaws.

Fargo rose to his feet, started forward in a long, loping crouch, and saw Titus and the four troopers go into action. Nokato, out of a flash of instinct, spun just as Fargo reached him, in time to take the butt of the Colt across the center of his forehead. As he collapsed, the other two turned. One caught the barrel of Titus's gun and the other a trooper's rifle butt. But the squaws had seen the attack and screamed and Fargo saw the old men running from both ends of the camp. "That's it. Hightail it," Fargo called out, and slung the inert form over his shoulder.

He reached the Ovaro, dumped the Indian across the saddle facedown, and saw one of the troopers do the same with a squaw. Holding Nokato in place with one hand, Fargo led the way along the back of the camp and heard the soft swishing sounds of arrows following. He veered into the deep woods, the sound of the rifle fire fading in the distance as the lieutenant retreated. Fargo continued to make a wide circle, moving as quickly as he dared through the blackness of the deep woods. It would still be dark when Red Claw returned, impossible for him to pick up their trail till morning. By the time dawn came they'd be well on their way back to the compound.

It had worked, he grunted in satisfaction. So far. But it was only a beginning. He had to make the rest work, match brutality with brutality, trickery with trickery, ignore all the civilized codes. And only Titus Toomey understood, because he knew the nature of the enemy.

7

"We made it back two hours ago. I'd been thinking that maybe it didn't go off," Lieutenant Baker said.

"You rode straight and fast. We sneaked in a long circle," Fargo said.

Baker looked at the woman as she was led away with Nokato and the others. "Why the squaw?" he asked.

"She was handy," Fargo grunted, and saw Devereaux looking on from outside his quarters.

"Nokato would have been enough. He'll exchange Bess for his brother," Devereaux said.

"Not until you prove yourself, this time," Fargo said.

"You saying I have to become as savage as Red Claw?" the major said.

"You're what you are. I'm saying I'm going to do whatever I have to do to try and save her and the others," Fargo answered, his eyes suddenly growing ice-cold. "You just be ready, Major. I expect Red Claw will be showing up soon." Fargo walked away and Titus followed as he found a quiet corner by the stables and lowered his long frame to the ground. "You know what it's going to be," he said to Titus. "You still with me?"

"A man starts something, he sees it through," Titus answered, and Fargo nodded gratefully as he closed his eyes. He'd slept for perhaps three or four hours, he estimated, when the shout woke him and he saw the trooper atop the stockade pointing into the distance. The major hurried across the yard to where Lieutenant Baker held his mount and Fargo swung onto the Ovaro.

"Just you and me," he said to Devereaux, and the major followed him out of the compound. Red Claw had halted his white pony just beyond the tree line. As Fargo reached the Indian, he took a grim satisfaction in the controlled rage that was plain on the stone face. "Nokato rides free now," the Arapaho chief barked.

"No," Fargo said, and saw the Indian's mouth tighten. "Free the girl and the others first."

"Nokato, now, or we kill one each day," Red Claw said.

"The major will kill one for each you kill," Fargo said. Red Claw let a derisive sound escape his lips as he turned his pony and rode away with slow deliberation. Fargo turned his horse and started back toward the compound.

"What was that all about?" Devereaux asked.

"He's going to make you prove you mean it," Fargo said.

"My God, man, you're playing with Bess's life," the major protested. "He could kill her first."

"No way. She's his ace card. Only now you have yours back," Fargo said.

"What next?" Devereaux asked.

"We wait. It's his move," Fargo said, and let the major hurry into the compound before him. Dark began to settle quickly and Fargo put his bedroll down in a corner near the stockade wall. Fatigue helped him to sleep quickly and when he woke with the early morning he washed inside the barracks and found Titus waiting for him when he came out.

"Devereaux and the lieutenant are up on the wall," Titus said. "The major looks like he hasn't slept much." Fargo grunted, began to climb the short flight of outside stairs that led to the platform along the top of the stockade and Titus clambered after him. Titus's observation had been very right, Fargo saw as the major turned a drawn, tense face at him, eyes red from sleeplessness and a fair amount of whiskey. Fargo leaned both arms atop the stockade fence and peered out to the thick stand of trees. The wait was a short one and he watched as the leaves moved at the first line of trees and the white pony came into sight, Red Claw sitting very straight atop it. He led another pony with the figure of a man draped facedown across its back in inert lifelessness.

"My God," Devereaux breathed as Red Claw left the pony and its silent burden standing in the open, turned his white pony, and disappeared back into the trees. Fargo spun away from the wall and met Titus's eyes.

"I'll take the first one," he said. "Get me a horse." He turned to the lieutenant, his face grim. "Come with me," he said, and hurried down the stairs. Baker caught up to him almost at the guardhouse and entered the building with him. "Unlock the cell door. You don't have to stay," Fargo said.

"I'll stay. I have to lock up again," the lieutenant said, and swung the barred door open. The four Arapahos inside the cell were on their feet, Nokato's face tight with contemptuous hate, the others stoically expressionless. But they all knew why he had come, Fargo realized. Perhaps they'd seen it in his eyes.

Perhaps because they knew what their chief would do. Perhaps it was the mysterious wisdom of the inner senses. But they knew.

Fargo felt the churning inside himself, distaste for what he had to do, a bitter sourness in the pit of his stomach. But Red Claw had felt none of that when he killed the hostage from the wagon train, Fargo reminded himself. He yanked the Colt out in one quick motion and the explosion of sound filled the small cell and the nearest Arapaho crumpled to the ground. Fargo immediately dragged the man outside as Baker locked the cell door, slung him across the horse Titus had waiting, and climbed onto the Ovaro.

He rode from the compound and across the open land with slow deliberation. When he reached the pony and the lifeless man the Arapaho had left, he let the reins of the other horse drop to the ground and grasped the rawhide lead of the Indian pony. Slowly, he started back toward the compound leading the pony and its lifeless rider. He glanced back as he heard the two braves come out of the trees, gather up the slain Arapaho, and make off with him. Fargo reached the compound where a crowd watched in silence, the major one of them, and he handed the rawhide reins to Baker. He turned and rode slowly from the compound, looked back when he heard the horse following, and saw Titus.

"You didn't come out just for a morning canter," the old guide remarked when he came alongside.

"Came to do some looking," Fargo said. "We'll need a hollow with good tree cover around it, someplace he can't see until he gets right up to it." Titus nodded and moved his brown mare to the east as Fargo started up a tree-covered slope of land. He disappeared into the trees and Fargo made his way slowly northward in the woods, scanning the forest land with a practiced eye when he heard the series of short whistles through the trees to his left. He turned the pinto and followed the sound until he saw Titus through the thick branches, went into a trot, and reined up where Titus waited at the edge of a hollow surrounded by shadbush.

"This do?" Titus asked.

"How far from open land?" Fargo queried.

"Couple dozen yards. I'll show you," Titus said, and led the way out of the woods. Fargo saw three flat, tablelike rocks in the open land as he emerged from the trees, halted, swept the nearby terrain with a slow glance, and took in a low rise nearby and the long line of blue spruce that ran north from it.

"This will do," he said. "I'll ride into those spruce now."

Titus's eyes crinkled at the corners. "Looking to set the way out in your mind?" he asked.

Fargo nodded. "There won't be much time. It'll be tricky and I figure I'll have maybe a minute head start. Maybe."

"You're convinced he'll pull something when the time comes?" Titus asked.

Fargo leveled a long gaze at the old guide. "You think different?"

Titus's lips pressed hard against each other. "No," he grunted. "Go find your way. I'll see you later."

Fargo put the Ovaro into a gallop and rode into the long line of blue spruce. He made his way inside the trees, keeping a steady pace as he made mental notes of every twisted trunk, every rotted log and woodland cluster of orange milkweed that could serve as a marker. When he finally finished, the sun had begun to slide down the afternoon sky and he made his way back to Owlshead. He reached town as night fell and found

Titus at the dance hall, answered the old guide's eyes with a nod, and enjoyed the bourbon Dolly brought.

"A lot of folks have got word to me that they're plenty worried. The major still talks about pulling out when they ask him," she said.

"Tell them nobody's pulling out," he said. "It's too late for that. He just doesn't know the truth of it." Dolly nodded gravely and Fargo ordered some buffalo meat well roasted and ate quickly when it came. He left Titus nursing another drink, found a corner in the compound, and drew sleep around himself, unwilling to think about what he knew the dawn would bring.

When the new sun sent its yellow-red fingers sliding across the morning sky, he woke, washed, and saw the major beside Lieutenant Baker atop the stockade. Fargo had just adjusted his gunbelt when he heard Devereaux's voice, a hoarse, quavering sound. "There he is," Fargo heard the major rasp. "Oh, my God. They've killed one of the women. Oh, good God."

Fargo started up the steps to the top of the stockade and halted beside Lieutenant Baker. He peered into the distance where he saw Red Claw on the white pony and, beside him, a horse with a gray-haired woman on it. She had been stripped naked and tied to the horse with lengths of rawhide so that she sat upright. Streaks of blood ran down her thighs, and from her breasts four arrows protruded, a line of blood trickling down each shaft. Her gray-haired head rolled lifelessly to one side and Fargo turned away to hurry down the steps to the ground. He saw Titus waiting and grimaced.

"I'll take this one," Titus said.

"The squaw," Fargo bit out, motioned to Baker, who hurried down and followed Titus to the jailhouse. Fargo strode to the stable and had just thrown a rope halter over one of the horses when he heard the single shot. Titus was waiting when he led the horse out, threw the lifeless body of the squaw onto the mount, and stepped back. Fargo pulled himself onto the Ovaro and rode from the compound with the second horse following. He retraced his steps of the morning before, left the horse with the squaw near the trees, and led the Indian pony with the woman on it back to the compound. He saw the two Arapahos come out to take the squaw away as he rode through the compound gate and swung to the ground while four troopers hurried up to cut the woman down.

"Filthy, Fargo, all of it filthy, despicable business," Devereaux hissed.

"It is," Fargo agreed with grim quietness.

"But you're going along with it, playing his game," the man accused.

"It's the only game in town now, Devereaux," Fargo snapped with sudden anger. "Thanks to you, Major." Devereaux spun away and strode to his quarters and Fargo led the Ovaro from the compound down main street.

"What next?" Titus asked as he caught up to him.

"Wait for tomorrow," Fargo said grimly. "I've done all the riding, looking, and getting ready I can do. There's only waiting left." He made a harsh sound. "That's always the hardest part," he said.

"Yep. How do you figure to do it?" Titus asked.

"Bourbon and a good bed," Fargo said. "Got any better ideas?"

"Nope," Titus said, and followed the big man into the dance hall. Fargo followed his own prescription for waiting with both discipline and vigor and he was stretched out on a bed in one of Dolly's rooms before the night grew long, happy to have the world closed away. When morning filtered through the lone window of the room, he woke with the added sourness in his mouth of too much bourbon and he washed and dressed quickly, hurried downstairs through the empty dance hall and out into the new day. He swung onto the Ovaro and rode fast and the trooper at the compound gate opened it for him. Behind him, Titus hurried along on the brown mare and Fargo found Devereaux and the lieutenant atop the wall. He dismounted and reached them just as Red Claw appeared leading a horse with another slain hostage draped across its back.

Fargo turned away at once, moved with quick, grim determination as the lieutenant followed him into the jailhouse. He saw the stoic, expressionless visage on the Arapaho and the contemptuous sneer on Nokato's face. "Your day's coming," he bit out in Sioux and the contempt disappeared from Nokato's face. Cursing inwardly, Fargo drew the Colt and fired, a single-death-dealing shot. The other Indian fell against the cell bars and slowly, almost reluctantly, slid to the ground.

"You are a dead man," Nokato hissed at Fargo.

"I won't be alone," Fargo snapped back, and dragged the other Arapaho from the cell while Baker slammed the door shut. Once again, he rode the Ovaro slowly out of the compound, leading the extra mount behind him to the edge of the trees. He brought the slain hostage back with him and Titus watched him return to the compound and slide from the saddle.

"Dolly's?" the old guide asked and Fargo nodded. "One more day, the hardest of them all," Titus said.

"Yes," Fargo agreed. "The rest were only waiting days. This will be a wondering day."

"He won't turn his back on Nokato, not after all this," Titus said.

"I don't think so, either, but he won't give in, not anymore," Fargo said. "He'll try to take Nokato and give us shit."

"You've been figuring on that. You've plans all made," Titus said.

Fargo nodded agreement as they pushed through the doors into the dance hall. "All I have to do is make them work," he said with bitter grimness, and welcomed the bourbon Dolly brought. He let the day slide away in bourbon and food and slept hard when night came, and before the dawn broke, he swung long legs over the edge of the bed, washed and dressed, and hurried to the compound.

He was atop the stockade wall when Devereaux joined him, the man's face tight with tension, all the arrogance gone from him. "You've pushed him too far, Fargo. You can't be sure what he's going to do," the major said tightly.

"Never said I was sure," Fargo muttered.

"I'm holding you responsible if it goes wrong," Devereaux said accusingly.

"That makes two of us," Fargo grunted, and felt his muscles grow taut as he saw the leaves move at the edge of the trees. The white pony slowly emerged from the trees, alone, no other pony following, and Fargo felt the silent explosion of relief inside himself. He turned and Devereaux hurried down the steps after him.

"I'm going with you," the major said, and Fargo shrugged as he climbed onto the Ovaro. He rode from the compound with Devereaux but a few paces behind him and slowed to a halt when he reached the waiting white pony. In the Arapaho chief's face he saw barely contained fury and the black-coal eyes burned with a dark fire.

"The girl for Nokato," Red Claw said.

Fargo met the Indian's burning, demanding stare. "The chief of the soldiers says the girl and all the others for Nokato," he answered.

Red Claw flicked a disdainful glance at Devereaux and returned the black-coal eyes to Fargo. "It is you who speaks now, tall one," the Arapaho said. "I knew inside myself it would come down to this, you and I."

"The girl and all the others," Fargo repeated, his voice made of steel. He watched the Arapaho chief's eyes narrow at him and saw the cunning behind the implacable hate. But the Indian knew there was no bluff, no idle bravado in the words that had been uttered. The past three days had proven that there'd be no shrinking back. His cold and merciless brutality had been matched.

"The girl and all the others for my brother," Red Claw muttered in sullen agreement.

"By the three flat rocks," Fargo said. "Just before the sun sets." The Indian nodded and turned his pony into the trees.

"Then we've an agreement," Devereaux said as he rode back to the compound with Fargo.

"We've shit," Fargo bit out, and drew a quick frown. "He won't keep it. It'll be a game of fox and hen."

"You mean you're not going to turn over Nokato?" the major asked.

"You get the cigar," Fargo said.

"Then he'll surely kill Bess," Devereaux protested.

"Not if things go the way I plan," Fargo said.

"I won't allow you to play with her life this way, Fargo," Devereaux said indignantly.

Fargo halted just outside the compound gate and fixed the man with an ice-blue gaze. "You won't allow?" he echoed. "You've nothing left to allow, mister. If I turn Nokato over to him, Bess and I will never make it back here alive. Now you ride on into your compound and keep on playing major but don't get in my way."

His face ashen, lips almost bloodless as they pressed

hard against each other, the man rode on and Fargo followed to halt beside the young lieutenant. "I'll want three horses an hour before sundown," he said, and rode on into town. He wasn't surprised to find Titus waiting for him at the dance hall.

"You set the wheels turning?" Titus asked, and Fargo nodded.

"Got a job for you," he said. "You stay close to Devereaux. If he takes it into his head to come charging out after I leave, you stop him. Tell him I told you to put a bullet into him if he sets one foot out of the compound."

"A pleasure." Titus grinned. Fargo patted the old guide's shoulder and went outside to climb onto the Ovaro. He rode through town, out at the south end, and found a shade tree. The day had turned hot and he let himself doze, went over his plan again, and waited for the day to slowly wind itself toward an end. He returned to the compound when the sun began to dip behind the distant purple bulk of Shadow Mountain, saw the major outside his quarters, pacing back and forth. Fargo smiled as he saw Titus lounging nearby and he put the Ovaro into a trot and rode across the open land leading the three horses the lieutenant had ready for him. He turned east when he caught sight of the long line of blue spruce and the sun had slipped behind Shadow Mountain when he reached the three flat rocks. He halted and his eyes were on the low rise to the right of the spruce when the white pony came into sight. At his side, Red Claw led a small pony and Fargo saw the flash of honey-wheat hair on the slender shape astride the pony. His eyes went past the Arapaho chief where a dozen braves came over the top of the rise with a big Conestoga. They halted and left the covered wagon atop the rise and followed Red Claw down the slope.

Fargo's gaze went to Bess as the Arapaho halted in front of him. Though her lovely, finely etched face was drawn, she seemed otherwise unhurt and her blue-gray eyes were clear, her gaze still strong. Fargo peered at the Indian and kept his own face expressionless. "Where are the others?" he asked.

"In the wagon," Red Claw said.

"Why?" Fargo asked.

"To make sure you would keep our agreement," the Arapaho said, and Fargo cursed silently. The answer was only half a lie and he didn't want to think about the other half.

"Where is Nokato?" Red Claw asked.

"In the hollow inside the trees straight behind you," Fargo said.

"Why?" the Arapaho questioned.

"To make sure you would keep our agreement," Fargo returned, and saw the Indian's eyes flicker for an instant. "I'll take the girl now," Fargo said.

"You bring Nokato out first," Red Claw said.

"You bring the wagon down here," Fargo said.

"You can go and bring it down yourself," the Indian said.

"Go to the hollow and find Nokato yourself," Fargo said, and felt the tiny beads of perspiration on the palms of his hands. Red Claw barked orders to the dozen braves and they turned their ponies and headed for the spruce. It would take them but a few minutes to find the hollow, Fargo realized, and he looked at Bess. "Get off and mount one of these horses," he said to her quietly. She slid from the bare back of the pony and quickly climbed onto one of the three extra horses he'd brought. Fargo moved the pinto forward, Bess at his side, and went into a trot as he took the long slope at a time-saving angle.

"I knew they were keeping me alive as a bargaining

tool," Bess murmured. "I just wondered how long that would last."

"Keep wondering," Fargo said. "You see any of the others inside the wagon?"

"No, they kept me separate," she said, and Fargo felt his lips draw back in a grimace as he reached the wagon. He went to the back and pulled the flap open and felt the bitter fury spiral through him. "Oh, good God," he heard Bess gasp from behind him as she came up and he stared at the bodies piled one atop the other inside the wagon, each with its throat slashed. He dropped the canvas flap as he muttered curses and the wild shout from the bottom of the slope broke into his bitter rage. He saw the dozen braves racing from the trees, shouting at Red Claw with excited gestures, and the Arapaho chief spun his white pony around.

"Ride!" Fargo shouted at Bess. "Ride like hell." He sent the Ovaro into a gallop, pulling the other two horses behind, and crested the rise and raced down the other side. Once on the back side of the slope, he veered sharply and raced into the long line of blue spruce. His eyes searching out every mark he had imprinted in his mind, he led the way in a series of short twisting turns, down a straight path and turning again, circling and racing on in the long forest of sweet-smelling spruce. He halted when he reached the stream, deeper and wider than most, that coursed through the forest. He tied the two extra horses together by their reins, slapped both sharply on their rumps, and sent them galloping across the stream and on through the woods. "This way," he barked at Bess as he rode into the stream and followed its course northward.

The forest was quickly darkening, he saw with satisfaction, and kept racing through the stream as the night blackness descended. The Arapahos would have time only to follow the prints of the other two horses for a few minutes before the night made further trailing in the woods impossible, and he slowed but continued to stay in the stream for another few hundred yards. Finally he pulled the pinto out onto the soft, dry land of the spruce forest. He found a place where a break in the trees allowed a shaft of moonlight to shine down and he slid from the saddle, reached arms out, and helped Bess from her horse. She stayed in his arms but there was no trembling in her and she finally pulled back. "I wondered if it'd be you come for me, finally," she said.

"Wondered or expected?" he asked.

"Where's my father?" she asked, turning the question aside.

"At the compound," Fargo said, and lowered himself to the bed of soft spruce needles. "Red Hawk will likely go back to his camp but I don't want to take any chances. We'll stay here till near dawn and then make our way back." Bess came down to sit beside him and he felt her eyes on him.

"How did you know what he'd do?" she asked.

"I didn't, not all of it, not about the wagon, damn him."

"But you figured the rest of it. How?"

"By seeing with his eyes, thinking with his mind, hating with his hate."

"You are something special," Bess said gravely.

"Flattery will get you almost anywhere." He grinned.

"It's funny, the things you think about when you don't know how long you have to live," Bess said. "You think about the things you should've done and didn't and about the things you'd do if you got a second chance."

"Such as?" Fargo said.

"Such as this," she said, and he felt her lips on his,

pressing softly, then with more strength until she pulled away, her face grave.

"You stop thinking there?" he asked mildly.

"No," she said, and he saw the faint smile touch her lips. He reached out, pulled her to him, and brought her mouth to his again, sweet honey taste, lips softly firm as they opened for him and he felt the softness of her tongue as it darted forward to meet his. "Oh, oh, yes, oh God, yes," Bess Devereaux murmured, and he felt the explosion inside her gathering itself. Her arms slid around his neck and her breasts pressed into his chest with warm softness. He undid buttons and she helped with the snap on her skirt without taking her lips from his. Her shirt came off and his hand moved over smooth, round shoulders and he pressed her down onto the soft carpet of the ground and took in the longish breasts, a slow, long curving line to them that filled out at the bottom with full, deep cups, each adorned by a pink circle and a deeper pink nipple. A flat abdomen led to a narrow waist, and straight hips and the curly black covering a pubic mound that rose in a provocative hill of flesh.

He took in nicely shaped legs, long thighs that avoided being thin by the fleshy curve that went into the narrow hips in a lovely, smooth line. He brought his lips down to one deep pink nipple and drew gently on it and Bess gave a tiny scream as her fingers dug into his back. "Ooooooh . . . aaaah," she moaned as he continued to gently suck, circle the erect tip with his tongue. "Ah, ah, aaaaaah," she continued to moan, and he let his hand drop down slowly over her body, exploring curves, touching, bringing his own warmth, and he saw her hips move, lift, fall back quickly. He took a moment to pull his own clothes off and when he'd done so he saw her eyes devouring him with wanting.

Bess reached up to him, her hands grasping his hips, moving down, brushing through his own black nap to curl around the pulsing maleness of him, and she uttered a half scream, half cry at the touch of him. "Please, oh please," she murmured against him, brought him against her flat belly, and pushed hard, reveling in the touch of his throbbing warmth against her flesh. "Take away the world, Fargo," she whispered. "For one night, this night, our night."

He nodded as his lips moved down across her belly and she cried out again and he saw the slender thighs come open, close at once and come open again. His hand came against the dark, warm portal with suddenness and Bess screamed at the touch of him and pushed her legs upward, opening the eternal entranceway as wide as she could. She made small crying sounds as he touched the glistening lips, pressed, explored, stroked. "Ah, ah, ah," Bess gasped with his every touch, lifting her hips, imploring with her body. She pulled at him with her hands until he came atop her, pressed himself over her and felt the quivering warmth of her. "Aaaaah, so good, so good," she breathed, and he felt her slender legs rubbing against his hips, pressing, rubbing again, each touch an entreaty of the flesh. "Please, please . . ." Bess whispered against him as her hips rose, moved in offering.

He rose, moved lower on her, and touched the tip of his throbbing maleness to her wet warmth and she gave a sharp cry, urging and anticipation in its sound. He moved forward, slowly, sliding into the moist tunnel, and Bess cried out as her hands dug into his back. "Oh, oh . . . ooooh, more, more . . . oh God, more," she murmured, and he felt the slender thighs come up to encircle his hips.

She surged upward with him and a deep groaning sound came from her, followed by another and still another as he drew back and forth inside the avenue of ecstasy. Moaning became softer, turned into sibilant soundings of pure pleasure, and Bess moved her body in rhythm with him, sliding her tight rear along the grass, then drawing back and sliding forward again. He found one of the longish breasts with his lips and drew it into his mouth and she cried out in pleasure as he sucked and caressed the soft, lovely mound. Suddenly Bess's moans grew longer, each one a deep, moaned cry that seemed never to end but to run into the other and he felt her legs stretch out and stiffen. The moaned sounds grew louder and longer and her body began to tremble. He saw the honey-wheat hair tossed wildly from one side to the other and between the moaned sounds he could distinguish gasped words.

"Yes . . . aaaaaoooo . . . yes . . . now, now . . . coming, oh God, oh God," Bess breathed, and her belly tightened, the slender thighs growing taut. The scream began as another moaned sound but rose in pitch until it was a breath-filled cry and then a scream. She quivered against him, her entire body stiffened, and he let himself explode with her and the tiny, warm contractions caressed him and he heard his own groan of pleasure.

Bess took one hand and pushed her left breast up for his lips and he pulled gently on it as, with a deep sigh that seemed to come from some inner cavern, she fell back onto the forest floor. Slowly her thighs stopped pressing into him but her hand on the back of his neck held his mouth to her breast until, with a final long sigh, she lay still. In the pale shaft of moonlight, the honey-wheat hair seemed a pale gold wreath and Bess Devereaux offered a slow and contented smile. "Shows what can come from thinking about something," she said.

"Maybe you'll get a chance to think some more

when this is over," Fargo said, and she rolled against him and brought one slender leg across his hips.

"Definitely," she said, and fell silent for a long moment. "Will we be here when it's over?" she asked.

It was his turn to pause. "I'm planning on it," he said finally.

"Good," she murmured, and fell asleep lying half over him. He slept in minutes, his arms wrapped around her slender body. The night stayed warm, the only sound that of the night insects when he suddenly snapped awake at her sharp cry. He had the Colt out of its holster alongside him instantly and saw Bess staring at him as she sat up, horror in her eyes. "Oh, God, I'm sorry," she said. "I'm sorry."

"What was it?" Fargo asked.

"All those poor people in the wagon, the sight of them came to me while I was asleep," she said. "I just screamed and woke up." She fell against him and held herself tight to him.

"It won't be the only time," Fargo told her. "Some things burn into the mind. Sometimes they never go away."

"This day will be one of them," Bess murmured, and lay down over him again, wrapped her legs around him and stayed tight against him. "And this night," she added as she returned to sleep. He closed his eyes again, slept with her until he woke with the moon far across the black velvet sky.

He stirred, pushed gently, and she woke with an effort. "Time to ride, honey," he said, and pulled her to her feet. He let her dress first and enjoyed the sight of it as the longish breasts swayed gently as she moved, leaned to the right, bent over, all the movements of dressing that became a study in sensuous motion. He pulled on clothes when she finished and led the Ovaro through the deep darkness of the forest. He took to the saddle as the trees thinned enough to let a little more of the waning moon's light into the woods.

"If we can reach open land before dawn we can make it to Owlshead. If not, we've got trouble. Red Hawk will have scouts out watching," Fargo said as he put the pinto into a trot. He kept the steady pace and cursed quietly as he watched the moon disappear from sight. He spurred the pinto into a gallop and Bess stayed close behind him as he neared the end of the long line of spruce.

When the first gray light of the new day began to paint the sky, tentatively at first, sliding up over the distant horizon, Fargo swore again as they were still in the trees. The early dawn light had come over the land when Fargo galloped out of the spruce onto open land, the three flat rocks to his right. He glanced back at Bess and saw she had fallen behind a half-dozen yards. Maybe they'd get lucky, he allowed himself to hope. Maybe the Arapaho scouts he knew would be watching all the land approaching Owlshead would still be just coming awake.

He was beginning to feel optimistic as the pinto raced across the open land, quickly shortening the distance to the town. Bess's mount managed to lose only another yard as he kept the hard-riding pace and he had just passed a cluster of hackberry when he saw the two riders appear from behind the trees. "Goddamn," he swore, and watched them fan out immediately. He pulled back on the Ovaro enough for Bess to catch up and swore again as he spotted the third Arapaho racing into sight from the left. "They'll be trying to take me out and take you alive," he shouted to Bess. "I'm going to let them think they hit pay dirt. You just keep riding like hell, understand?"

She nodded and Fargo held the Ovaro back and let her race ahead. The three Arapaho were closing in fast. Two carried rifles, one a bow, he saw, and he bent low in the saddle as he drew the big Sharps from its saddle case. The two on his right were within range of him and he sat up, saw them raise their rifles, and dropped low in the saddle again.

Their first round of shots was wild and he veered the pinto to the side. The second volley whistled over his head and he yanked hard at the reins as he let himself fall from the saddle. He hit the ground, clutching the rifle to his stomach, and lay still and heard the whoops of triumph as the two braves charged on after Bess. He kept his head down, listened, and heard the third one pass a half-dozen yards ahead. Slowly he raised his head and saw the three braves were almost abreast of Bess and he swung the rifle from under his body, brought it to his shoulder, and took aim. His first shot sent the Arapaho closest to Bess spinning off his pony. The rider nearest him turned to look back and took Fargo's second shot full in the chest. He stayed on his racing pony for a moment, bobbing up and down while red sprayed from his chest as though he were a fountain gone berserk.

Fargo swung the big Sharps around to draw a bead on the third brave but he saw the Indian dive from his pony and land on Bess's back. She fell from her horse with the man clinging to her and Fargo leaped to his feet and ran forward. The Arapaho got up first and yanked her to her feet, spun her around so that he held her in front of him, and Fargo saw the bone knife he pressed to her throat.

"Throw gun over here," the Indian said in Sioux, and Fargo hesitated. The Arapaho pressed the knife harder into Bess's throat. "Over here. Now," he demanded and Fargo swore silently. He threw the rifle so that it landed some six feet away from the Arapaho and silently hoped the Indian would make a dive for it. But the man was not about to make that mistake and he dragged Bess with him as he moved sideways toward the rifle.

Holding on to Bess, the Indian bent over carefully, reached one arm out to pick up the rifle, and Fargo's hand rested on the butt of the Colt on his hip. The Arapaho's fingers closed around the stock of the rifle, Bess still held in front of him. He'd have the Sharps up to fire in another two seconds and Bess still his shield. With a curse, Fargo yanked the Colt from its holster and fired two shots at the brave's hand as it closed around the rifle still on the ground. Both bullets slammed into the dirt, one so close it nicked the edge of the stock. The Arapaho's reaction was instant and automatic as he jerked his hand away, for a second concerned only with avoiding the bullets. Bess caught the momentary distraction and flung herself down and out of his grasp. As she hit the ground, Fargo brought the Colt up. The Arapaho reached down to push the knife against her neck but Fargo's shot struck him in the left breast and he toppled over backward as though he'd been poleaxed.

Bess was already pushing herself to her feet, Fargo saw. "Mount up. Let's get out of here before we've more company," he said, and ran back to the Ovaro. He vaulted into the saddle and had the horse at a full gallop in seconds. His eyes swept the nearby hills and slopes as they raced on but no other bronze-skinned horseman appeared and he allowed himself a deep breath of relief as the town came into sight, the compound gate swinging open. He rode in and reined to a halt, saw Titus waiting, and smiled as the old guide nodded at him approvingly. Devereaux rushed from his quarters to fling his arms around Bess and Fargo swung to the ground beside Lieutenant Baker.

"We found the wagon," the lieutenant said. "When

you didn't come back, the major sent out a squad. We dug a mass burial site."

"Fargo," he heard Bess call. "I'm going to wash and change and rest some. Will you come by later?" He nodded and watched her hurry away and found himself thinking about the honey-wheat passion of her.

"I owe you a debt of gratitude, Fargo," the major said, breaking into his thoughts. "But we still have Nokato. Red Claw's not going to sit by for that."

"He'll take another wagon train of hostages and try again," Baker said.

"No. He knows the rules have changed," Fargo said pointedly, and saw Devereaux's lips thin.

"We just wait for his next move?" Baker queried.

"You do what you should've done in the first place, put Nokato in front of a firing squad," Fargo snapped.

"Absolutely not," Devereaux cut in. "You stooped to Red Claw's brutal barbarism. I told you I won't be a party to it. A proper trial will be held when the federal judge gets here."

"Red Claw isn't going to wait. You kill Nokato or ship him out of here. But get rid of him. Red Claw won't waste braves on something that's past changing," Fargo said.

"There's a judge and federal prison in Rangeville just by the Utah border," Baker said. "But we don't have enough troopers to get him there. The Arapaho will attack with everything they have."

"I think there's a way. You have a closed prisoner wagon?" Fargo asked.

"Yes, sir," the lieutenant said.

"I say we just wait for the federal judge to arrive. We've enough men to defend the compound from a direct attack," Devereaux said.

"Maybe and maybe not. He's got more men and all those nice rifles you gave him," Fargo said. "The only answer you have is to get rid of Nokato, one way or the other. If you won't shoot him or hang him because you want to play civilized, then ship him out. Otherwise, all hell's going to break loose."

"Stop by this evening, Fargo. I'll consider this," Devereaux said. Fargo smiled at the answer, a face-saving reply, meant more for the lieutenant than anyone else. Fargo strolled away, the Ovaro following behind him, and Titus fell into step alongside.

"Want to fill me in on tomorrow?" Titus asked.

"At Dolly's," Fargo said. "Over some breakfast." Titus sat down across from him when they reached the saloon and Dolly served them hot coffee and scrambled eggs with thick rye bread. She left them alone as Fargo told the old guide everything he planned, and when he finished he sat back and waited as Titus thought in silence.

"It can work," the old guide said at last. "But you're risking losing half of the major's men."

"Not if Devereaux sticks to the plan," Fargo said.

"If," Titus said.

Fargo frowned, "No reason for him not to."

"Men like the major come up with their own reasons when you don't want them to. But we'll hope for the best," Titus said, and Fargo rose and felt the tiredness sweep over him.

"I'm going to sleep some," he said.

"I'm sure you can use it," Titus said as Fargo followed Dolly to a room at the top of the stairs. He lay across the bed and slept at once and it was dark when he woke. He rinsed his face with water in the big white basin on the dresser and went downstairs where the saloon was already crowded with customers. He made his way to the compound and saw the moon was almost full. When he walked into Devereaux's quarters, he found Lieutenant Baker waiting also. He quickly outlined his plan in detail and saw Baker nod under-standing and agreement as he went through each part.

The major's arrogant tolerance no longer irritated him, its hollowness transparent. "You'll lead the main detail," Fargo said to Devereaux. "It's important Red Claw see you. He'll expect you to be in charge of a move as important as this."

"Naturally," Devereaux said.

"You'll pick your six best men," Fargo said, turning to the lieutenant. "And get everything else ready."

"Yes, sir," the lieutenant said crisply.

"That's it, then," Fargo said, and got to his feet. He left the room wondering why he felt a sudden rush of uneasiness, and when he reached the dark outside he saw the slender figure leaning against a post. She came over to him at once and her lips pressed against his.

"I told Father Emily Kroger asked me to come visit," she said. "I want an hour alone with you before tomorrow."

"Why not?" Fargo grinned.

"There are guest quarters at the back of the com-pound. They're empty," she said, and he followed her along the deep shadows at the edge of the supply shed to a small building set off to one side. She pushed the door open and in the dim moonlight that came through the lone window he saw a large bed and nightstand beside it, a wood dresser against one wall and a lamp on it. Bess crossed to the bed with quick strides and whirled, lifted the dress she had on with one, swirling motion, and was naked in front of him. He pulled off clothes as she sank onto the bed, stretched out, and reached her arms up for him.

"You've been thinking again," he said as he sank down over her and felt the warmth of her skin, its own kind of embrace.

"Yes, thinking and wanting," she murmured, and

her mouth found his, open, hungry, demanding. He met her tongue with his, pressed hard against her lips, and felt her body move under his, her thighs coming open at once. He brought his mouth down to the long, full-cupped breasts and pulled on each, gently first, then harder, and Bess murmured sounds as she pressed upward against him. He let his mouth move down across her flat abdomen, his tongue a lapping trail of warm desire, halting at the tiny, round indentation in her belly to circle it slowly, reach into its shallow darkness, and Bess cried out in delight and her thighs opened wider and came together to slap against his side.

He let his hands move slowly across the narrow hips, caressing gently, flattening down over the small nap-covered pubic mound, and she cried out again in pleasure. He moved back, brought one hand down to cup the warm wet place between her legs, and the tiny, straying wisps of soft-wire hair rested against his palm.

"Oh, oh, oh, yes, yes . . . oh, don't stop, please," Bess gasped out, and her pelvis lifted entreatingly. He let his fingers move over the soft spot of feverish pleasure and Bess screamed out, a sudden explosion of ecstasy beyond ecstasy, and as he continued to caress the dewy tip he heard her gasped words. "You . . . you . . . you'll make me come, oh, God, oh God, Fargo," she said, and he felt her legs tremble against him. He rose, brought his own wanting organ quickly to her, and thrust forward, groaned in the pleasure of it as he slid through her warmth and Bess brought her hands around his neck, pulled his face into her breasts.

He felt her tremble, on the very brink of that final explosion of ecstasy, but she managed to hold back as she reveled in the excruciating pleasure of his slow thrustings inside her. "Yes, oh yes, yes, yes," she breathed, moved with him, and continued to draw upon her self-discipline to hold back the moment of climax. But the pleasure mounted upon itself, the body's delight climbing beyond all control of the mind, and the deep moaning sound tore from her as she rose under him and he felt her quivering contractions explode around him. Her moaning cry came from some wellspring of passion so deep it engulfed the world and all that was part of it in one encompassing moment. The cry rose, turning from a moan into a groan of ecstasy and protest as the moment began to vanish with the same uncontrollable power that brought it to eruption.

She sank back on the bed, suddenly all softness, and her thighs fell from his sides almost as if in defeat. "Oh, my God, Fargo," she murmured. "Why can't it last longer?"

"Maybe if it lasted longer, we wouldn't," he said as he lay beside her, and she curled against him. She lay silent with her body wrapped around his until finally she sat up and he enjoyed the slender loveliness of her.

"I'd best get back," she said, and he heard the reluctance in her voice.

"I'll come for you in the morning," he said, and the gray-blue eyes filled with surprise.

"I'll want you riding with me," he said. "I'm going to be watching from a distance but I want you with me." Her frown prodded and he answered as he began to dress. "I expect things to go just as I planned. But the compound will have less than half the troopers in it. If Red Claw does decide to pull a surprise, I want you with me, not here."

"I'll be waiting," she said as she disappeared under the folds of the dress she pulled over her head. He rose, strapped on his gunbelt, and left the little building with her, then watched her go on back to Devereaux's quarters. He retrieved the Ovaro a few moments later and rode back through the mostly silent town and halted at the saloon. Inside, Titus sat at one of the tables and Fargo slid into the chair beside him, ordered a bourbon, and let thoughts slowly parade through his mind. He saw Titus fasten him with a crinkled glance of shrewd appraisal.

"Wondering if it's going to work?" Titus asked.

"Yes and I've no right to do that now," Fargo said.

"Why not?" Titus frowned. "A man can always wonder."

"No, there's no time left for wondering. The cards are all dealt. There's nothing left but to play them," Fargo said, and downed the bourbon with a rush of grimness.

8

He stayed on the high land where the tree cover was heavy and he could see the double column of troopers making their way below. Bess stayed close at his side as he slowed and watched the column move across a stretch of open land. The major rode at the head of the column, the lieutenant behind him, and in the center of the line of blue-coated riders, the tightly closed, high-sided prison van, a driver and a guard with it. He was not the only one that watched the procession move swiftly across the land, Fargo knew. Red Claw's scouts had seen it and quickly sent word and he cast a glance at the sun that had moved high in the sky. "Plenty of time," Fargo muttered with a frown.

"For what?" Bess questioned.

"For Red Claw to have reached here with his main force. He's holding back," Fargo said. "Let's ride some," he added, and sent the Ovaro into a canter. He maneuvered through the trees, stayed on the high land, and moved ahead of the column below to pull up sharply when he reached a long sloping hillside. He pointed to a long, narrow passageway below, almost a small valley. "There's the reason," Fargo said grimly.

"He wants the column in that valley before he attacks." Fargo lifted his gaze to sweep both sides of the sloping hills but the tree cover was thick, mostly hackberry and elm with heavy foliage that offered only a green curtain. He saw the fear in Bess's face as she stared down at the valley.

"They'll be all right," he said. "There's plenty of room for them to turn the wagon."

She frowned. "What's that mean?"

"I'll explain later," Fargo said as he saw the column start to ride into the valley. He moved the Ovaro forward into a thicket of high shrubs and shadbush that offered a better view of the valley and a better hiding place. He felt the frown dig into his brow as the column moved along below, well into the valley now, and the hills continued to stay quiet. Devereaux had almost reached the other end of the valley where the land opened up into a plateau when both slopes erupted, the trees disgorging a horde of near-naked riders. They emerged in silence at first and as they gathered speed and raced downhill the air filled with their wild whooping cries.

Fargo saw Devereaux rein up and ride back to his troopers. It was too far away to hear the orders the major barked but he saw the column break ranks and deploy in two lines on each side of the closed wagon, one line facing the east slope, the other the west. "What the hell is he doing?" Fargo bit out as he saw the troopers hold their places and start to exchange fire with the Arapahos that charged down the hillsides at them. "Jesus Christ, he's making a stand," Fargo almost yelled. "He's making a goddamn stand."

"What did you expect him to do, surrender?" Bess asked accusingly.

"Turn and run, goddammit. That was the plan," Fargo barked. "I knew he'd be outnumbered and outgunned. He was to turn and run with the van, fight a defensive action while they ran." Fargo winced as he saw the blue-uniformed figures begin to fall from their horses as the Arapahos raced back and forth, moving fast, firing in clusters as they rode. "Goddamn him," Fargo shouted, and pounded his fist against the side of a tree. "Goddamn his stinking soul."

"Maybe he decided there was no time to make a run for it," Bess said, her voice tight as she stared in horror at the carnage that had erupted below.

"There was time and there was room. That was the whole goddamn idea. He was to run and he'd lose only a handful of men. Now they're a stationary target, sitting ducks," Fargo said.

"He was to run all the way back to the compound with the Arapaho chasing after him?" Bess frowned.

"He was to make a run for it, then let the van go and race like hell away," Fargo said. "Red Claw would have gone after the van and broken off the chase."

"All this to just give up Nokato?" Bess asked.

"Nokato's not inside the van," Fargo said. "He's on his way to Rangeville with six troopers. They sneaked out last night with him, went south through town in a wide circle along the Sweetwater River. This was all set up to give them more of a clear start."

Fargo saw Bess stare at him as the bitterness welled up in her eyes and he turned back to the scene below. He spotted the lieutenant and some of the other troopers as they turned their horses and started to run for it. There weren't more than a handful left out of over fifty, he saw, and watched three more of those go down. But Red Claw waved his braves back as he rode to the wagon and Fargo watched him break the locked rear door in with a tomahawk.

He saw the Arapaho chief stop, step back, and lift his head to the sky. His scream of rage carried all the way up to the thicket and seemed to shake the hills. Fargo's eyes moved slowly across the blue-uniformed figures that lay strewn across the ground and halted as he found Devereaux, his army-issue Colt dragoon pistol still in his hand. "Damn you," he bit out. "Damn your gutless soul."

"You can't say that now," Bess flung at him, her voice breaking. "He died trying to stand up to them. That's not weak."

"There's a time when it's strong to be weak and weak to be strong. He didn't have the guts to stand fast when he should have and he didn't have the guts to run when he should have," Fargo said harshly, unwilling to let her turn away from the truth once more. He looked past her down into the valley and saw Red Claw striding through the slain troopers, his tomahawk in hand. He searched for Devereaux, Fargo realized, and knew what he'd do when he came on the man.

He yanked Bess's mount around by the cheekstrap and hurried out of the thicket and rode up onto higher land and into the trees where the valley was blocked from sight. He kept moving and heard the deep sobs that came from her as she followed. When he reached a high place where the land wound down in a narrow trail on the back side of the hill, he halted. She had stopped the bitter sobs but the pain was stark in the gray-blue eyes. He had no word that would help, he knew, and he let her slowly ride in silence until he halted at a stream. He slid from the saddle and let the horses drink and heard Bess come up to him. She leaned into his arms, held on to him but there was only a quiet sadness in her voice when she spoke. "You were right that very first time," she said.

"When was that?" he asked.

"When you told me to go home," she murmured. "How did you know then? Why were you so sure?"

"Trails and signs," he said, and she waited. "They're in a man's face, in his eyes and his ways, just as surely as they're in the roads and fields. Same for a woman."

"What trails are in my face, Fargo?" she asked.

"New ones," he said. "New pains, new depths. In time they'll make you more beautiful." She thought about his words and made no reply and he helped her onto her horse.

"It is over now?" she asked as he started forward.

"No," he said. "Let's make time. I want to get back." He put the Ovaro into a trot and made a long circle around the hills until he threaded his way back to the open land in front of the compound. The twilight had turned to night when he rode into the compound with her and saw Titus standing beside the lieutenant, who wore a bandage around a scalp wound.

"I heard," Titus grunted.

"You were right. He came up with his own stinking reasons," Fargo said.

"Titus says Red Claw will attack," the lieutenant cut in.

"He will. He's not only mad as all hell but he knows you've only a few dozen men left. Maybe if we had a full troop, he'd eat his fury but not now. He's got a chance to wipe every one of us out and he's going to take it," Fargo said.

"We'll bring everyone in town in. That'll give us at least another twenty or thirty rifles," Baker said.

"That'll still leave him with over twice as many warriors," Fargo said. "I've been thinking hard on it all the way back here. We're going to need more, some advantage that'll let us pick them off instead of trying to fight a pitched battle with them."

"You come up with anything?" Titus queried.

"Want to sleep on it," Fargo said. "I figure we have a day left. The Arapaho will give themselves another night to work themselves up with war dances and medicine man rituals."

"See you come morning," Titus said, and Fargo smiled at the old guide.

"You assume a lot," Fargo said.

"Nope. I know a woman with a waiting look in her eye when I see one," Titus said, and hurried away. Fargo walked to Devereaux's quarters and Bess turned from the window to put her arms around him.

"I just want not to be alone tonight," she said. He nodded understanding and she led him into her room, undressed, and waited for him to finish. She climbed into the bed with him and laid her slender softness against him in silence until he heard the steady sounds of sleep in her breathing. He lay awake and his mind revolved with thoughts before he finally closed his eyes in sleep until the brightness of the morning sun filtered through the window. He woke and swung from the bed and he'd washed and dressed when Bess sat up, her face grave. "Thank you," she said softly. "For understanding, for just holding me."

"There's a time for doing and a time for waiting," he said, and hurried from the room. Outside, Titus leaned against a post and he saw the lieutenant with a fresh bandage on his head.

"I was thinking maybe we ought to clear out," the lieutenant said. "Take everybody in town with us."

"They'd come after us and pick us apart like hawks raiding a chicken house," Fargo said. "We've got to stay but turn things in our favor. Red Claw will hit the compound first. He'll expect we will have brought everyone in town into the compound."

"Which is what we'd have to do," Baker said.

"So he'll fight his way in and go through every building in the compound to massacre every living soul he can find," Fargo said. "When he's finished, he'll burn down the town and kill anyone that might still be there. So we'll turn that around. We'll do the burning."

"How's that?" Titus asked, straightening up.

"You've got to have a good supply of kerosene and oil on hand," Fargo said to the lieutenant. "Kerosene for lamps, for cleaning, oil for softening riding gear, and maybe grease for wagon wheel work."

"We do, plenty of all three," Baker said.

"Get out every bit you can find. We're going to coat the base of the entire stockade, every building and shed inside the compound. When they've charged in and start rampaging through the buildings we'll set it all on fire. This old wood will go up like kindling, inside, outside, and all around them," Fargo said.

"They'll come running out and we'll be waiting outside to pick them off as they come out," Titus said. "They won't be able to go back without being burned alive and we'll keep pouring lead into them. The fire will take care of those that stay inside and we can take most of those who try to escape. By damn, I think it'll work."

"One thing, Fargo," Baker said. "They'll see us waiting outside when they come up. It's all open land."

"We won't be waiting outside. Every one of your men will be inside a house in town," Fargo said. "Soon as the flames shoot up they come out running, hit the ground, and start firing."

"All right," the lieutenant said, and Fargo glanced at him sharply. The smooth-cheeked, young face hadn't changed any but the man behind it had. Lieutenant Baker was still the same age outside but he had grown up inside. "I'll have all you need brought out. I'll set ten troopers to coating everything in the compound."

"Titus, you go get the townsfolk here and tell them what we're doing and what we expect of them," Fargo said. He turned to a corporal who had been standing by. "Have the men take their extra uniforms, all their personal things, and start moving everything into town. The same for equipment that you'll want to keep. Tonight, take the horses all the way to the end of town. There's an old granary shed there. Clean the clutter out of it and put the horses inside."

"Yes, sir," the soldier said, and hurried away. Fargo turned and saw Bess in the doorway, watching with her face grave.

"You'll be going with the others tonight?" he said.

"And you? Won't you be going to town to wait?" she asked.

"No," he said. "Somebody's got to light the bonfire." He saw the protest leap into her eyes and walked away. There was more than lighting the fire but that was reason enough for her. He saw the lieutenant starting to supervise the troopers as they began coating the base of the barracks and walked over to him. "You've some extra rifles still left, I hope," he said, and Baker nodded. "I want a dozen of them wedged into the spaces at the top of the stockade. Angle them downward and wedge them in tight. We've got to make it seem like we're in here firing back."

"Yes," Baker agreed. "You figuring to stay in here and run from rifle to rifle until they start breaking in and then set the fire."

"That's right," Fargo said. "Once the fire starts, it'll leap from place to place. This soaked wood will be blazing in less than a minute."

"You still can't do it alone," the lieutenant said.

"You volunteering, Lieutenant?" Fargo asked.

"I am," Baker said. "I've some making up to do, Fargo. I should've stood up to Devereaux with you. I should've taken command back there in that valley. I should've seen through the man."

"He was your commanding officer. They don't train

147

you to look past that uniform, soldier," Fargo said. "Don't eat at yourself and I'm glad for the help." He saw the lieutenant smile, a wry, almost sad smile, and he realized something. "First time I've seen you smile, Lieutenant," he said.

"Might be the last time," Baker said.

"Might be. No sense in lying to you," Fargo said. "Now let's get back to work. Give me one of those brushes and a bucket of that grease." Baker handed him a wooden bucket and Fargo began to soak the bottom sides of the barracks. It was hard, boring work but the hours went by and he halted as dusk drew itself down and Titus came by.

"Had everyone meet outside Dolly's place. They all know what's expected of them. The women and children will stay back but the men will follow the troopers out when the time comes," Titus said.

"Good. Stick around and help move the horses into what you used to call home," Fargo said. He stepped back and watched as the troopers began to move their mounts in pairs from the compound and down through the town. The lieutenant followed as he climbed the steps to the top of the stockade and moved along the line of rifles that had been wedged into place.

"All loaded and ready to fire," Baker said. Fargo nodded and went down the steps as Bess came from the major's quarters carrying her traveling bags.

"I won't sleep, not till it's over," she said gravely. "Not till you hold me again."

"Keep the faith, honey," he said, and watched her walk into the darkness. The last of the troopers filed from the compound and the lieutenant pulled the gate closed. The sounds from outside faded away and the compound grew still and silent. As silent as a morgue, Fargo grunted inwardly. "Get some sleep," he said to the lieutenant. "They won't attack till daylight."

Baker followed him to the top of the stockade where he lay down and stretched out and drew sleep around himself. But his sleep was the sleep of the mountain lion, every instinct alert under the blanket of slumber, the body asleep but the senses ever awake. But the night stayed quiet and when morning came he woke, pushed himself onto one knee, and peered over the top of the stockade fence. The open land was empty and nothing moved in the distant trees.

Baker woke and Fargo let him go down to wash the sleep from his face. When the lieutenant returned to stand sentry, Fargo went down to the major's quarters and washed. He made coffee on a small stove and brought a tin mug up to Baker. "One last thing to do if we want a chance to get out alive," he said as he finished his coffee. "You keep watch and I'll take care of it." He hurried down to the stable and returned with three coils of rope. He slung the first over the top of one side wall of the stockade fence, the second over the rear wall, and the third onto the other side wall. He let the end of each rope hang loosely, almost touching the ground. "Pick whichever one you like when the time comes," he called up to Baker as the lieutenant watched him.

"You can most surely count on that," Baker answered. He glanced over the top of the fence and Fargo saw his body stiffen and he sent long legs racing up the steps before the lieutenant found his voice. He peered across the open land to where the double line of horsemen had come from the tree cover. As he watched, another double line of bronzed figures rode into sight and he saw the white pony. The Arapahos sat unmoving on their horses, a menacing line of power held in check. Not a brave moved and the minutes began to seem like hours. Fargo glanced across at the lieutenant and saw the little beads of perspiration glisten on his face. Then, as one, the Arapahos turned and faded back into the trees.

"What's that mean?" Baker asked. "They change their minds about attacking?"

"Not likely," Fargo said.

"Then why'd they leave?" Baker pressed.

Fargo's lips pursed as he replied. "I'm not sure yet," he said. "Relax. We've nothing to do but wait and see." Baker took out a kerchief and wiped his face with it while Fargo slouched against the stockade fence. He estimated that a little over an hour had gone by when the Arapahos emerged from the trees again, this time in clusters of horsemen that halted as Red Claw barked a command. They had come a dozen yards closer, Fargo saw as they stayed in place until, at another command, they turned and raced back into the trees.

"What are they doing, dammit?" the lieutenant swore.

"Trying to put us on edge," Fargo said. "Remember, they think there's a troop of soldiers here. If there were, you can bet that a lot of them would be climbing the walls by now."

"How many more times are they going to do this?" Baker said.

"Maybe a lot. Maybe that was it. They've got you rattled already," Fargo said, and the lieutenant swallowed hard.

"I get the message," he muttered, and drew in a deep breath. When he positioned himself at the nearest rifle he had gathered himself in, Fargo saw approvingly. The sun had begun to hang high in a noon sky and Fargo let his big frame sink down to the platform. He rested, let his eyes close and his wild creature hearing explore the silence. A covey of bobwhite clucked in the distance and he heard a yellow warbler's bright song. A soft warm wind brushed the high grass with a sibilant sound and the morning seemed utterly peaceful. The smile that touched his lips was edged with wry bitterness. Red Claw understood the power of mounting tension and he was using it well.

"Bastard," he heard the lieutenant mutter, and Fargo opened his eyes and pushed himself to his feet. He had just straightened up when the trees erupted, this time in an explosion of wildly charging horsemen. They came in clusters of a dozen, fanning out, and Fargo saw a set of braves carrying a length of log between them to use as a battering ram. No fake charge, Fargo saw, and picked out the white pony at the head of a band that came in from the right.

"Fire," Fargo shouted as the racing horsemen came into range. He pressed the trigger of the rifle in front of him, stayed low, and ran to the next, fired off a round there, and went on to the next rifle. He glanced back and saw Baker doing the same with the line of rifles at his end of the stockade, firing and racing in a crouch to the next, then back again. Fargo retraced steps, firing a round from each rifle as he went, then raced back again to repeat the pattern. He paused for an instant to peek over the top of the stockade wall and ducked down as a hail of bullets slammed into the wood to send up a shower of splinters. The heavy barrage of bullets continued to splinter the top of the stockade fence and Fargo heard the sound of the log being smashed into the gate.

"Keep firing," he shouted at Baker. "They're trying to set up a covering barrage while they take the gate." He squeezed off another round from the nearest rifle and ran to the next. Perhaps some of the bullets struck a target, perhaps none of them did. It didn't matter. All that mattered was that the attackers continued to think there was a defensive force fighting back.

He saw Baker on one knee, half crawling, half running, from gun to gun as he kept his head down. The sharp sound of splintering wood echoed up through the gunfire and Fargo saw the log batter its way through the gate. Another blow and the gate would give way entirely, he knew. He saw the lieutenant cast a nervous glance downward. "Keep firing, dammit," he barked, and Baker returned to the rifles. Fargo raced along his part of the wall, firing off short bursts with each rifle, and spun as he heard the sound of the gate give way. "All right, run for it," he shouted at Baker and yanked one of the rifles from where it was wedged into the fence.

He followed Baker down the steps to the ground and saw the first of the attackers start to leap his horse over the base of the smashed gate. On long legs, he quickly outraced Baker to the rear of the compound and yanked some long wooden matches from his pocket. He struck the first and tossed it against the base of the barracks. A sheet of flame shot up instantly, spread lengthwise along the building with frightening speed. He glanced at Baker and saw the lieutenant had set one wall afire, and again he saw the flames spread with furious speed.

A sheet of flame leaped across the space between the barracks and the supply shed to send the other building up in an explosion of fire. But the Arapahos were pouring through the gate and into the compound, charging wildly, and Fargo saw the lieutenant crouched against the edge of the front wall of the stockade as he tossed two matches onto the kerosene-soaked wood. Two Arapahos spotted him, swerved their mounts, and raced toward him and Fargo drew a bead on the first and fired. The Indian toppled from his sight and he smashed a bullet into the second brave as he came into his sights. The Arapaho flew sideways from his horse as the bullet slammed into his ribs.

Baker was racing back in a crouch as the wall behind him erupted in a flame that shot lengthwise as it rose upward. Fargo squeezed the trigger of the rifle at three Arapahos who raced toward him and heard only the click of an empty chamber. He flung the gun away, yanked the Colt out, and fired off three shots. The first two riders fell and the third veered away. The odor of burning oil and kerosene filled the air and the clouds of smoke began to billow upward. The heat had suddenly become intense as the compound buildings all caught fire and Fargo heard the sound of rifle fire outside the front gate and just beyond the now furiously burning fence. He glimpsed the Arapahos, most all of them, milling around in the center of the compound, and with a quick glance behind him he saw that the last section of the rear fence had begun to flame.

"That's it. Run for it," he yelled to Baker, and the lieutenant, who was nearer to the wall, grabbed the rope and began to pull himself up along the fence. Fargo spied two Arapahos on foot racing between flaming buildings toward the rear fence. They spotted Baker near the top of the stockade, started to bring their rifles up to fire, but Fargo let go with three shots in quick succession.

Both Indians stumbled forward as they fell and struck the ground almost on top of one another and Fargo threw a glance up at the fence in time to see Baker disappear over the top. But the bottom of the last wall was blazing and Fargo holstered the empty Colt as he raced forward, his long legs carrying him to the fence in a half-dozen strides. The bottom of the rope had already begun to burn and Fargo cursed silently as he gathered himself, pressed down on steel-spring thigh muscles, and leaped upward.

His hands closed on the rope but he felt the flames

curling at his legs, reaching fiery fingers up to consume what they could. He drew his legs up and pulled hard on the rope, lifting himself upward until he could brace his feet against the wood. He pulled again, made quick progress now and clambered over the top of the fence. He took enough of the rope with him to help lessen the fall and landed on the balls of his feet and felt the jarring impact go through his body. He saw Baker pulling himself along the ground, dragging his left leg, and he caught up to the lieutenant. "Twisted my knee when I landed," Baker hissed. "I'll make it."

Fargo nodded and raced forward. The compound was an inferno now, flames shooting high into the air, the stockade fence a four-sided wall of fire. Fargo reached the corner and dropped to one knee. Three lines of troopers lay flat on the ground a dozen yards from the compound, a sprinkling of men from the town among them, and he saw the ground near what had been the gate strewn with Arapahos. But the attackers were still leaping through the flames to get out, and while some raced away alive, more fell victim to the direct barrage of bullets from outside.

"We did it." He chortled as the lieutenant limped up. "By God we did it." But as he spoke, a cluster of riders, perhaps eight or more, raced through the flame-shrouded gate and veered sharply to the right. Fargo saw at least four fall to the withering barrage, then another two go down, but he saw the white pony racing away, its rider bent low. "No, damn him, he's not going to get away," Fargo hissed, rose to his feet, and raced to where one of the Indian ponies had halted.

He vaulted onto the horse's saddleless back, pressed his legs tight against the animal's sides, and raced after the fleeing white pony. He saw Red Claw glance back as he went into the trees and Fargo kept the pony charging when he reached the trees. He flattened his long body across the pony, his head resting against the side of the horse's powerful neck. The shot sent a shower of wood chips from a tree just inches from his head and Fargo let himself slide sideways from the horse, hit the ground on all fours, and rolled as another shot slammed into the tree.

Behind a low bush, he turned and saw the white pony ride into view. Red Claw spied him at once, raised the rifle, and pressed the trigger and Fargo heard only the empty click. With a roar, the Arapaho leaped from his mount and landed on both feet on the ground. Fargo rose and his hand went to the holster when he realized there'd been no time to reload. Red Claw wasn't about to give him the time now, he saw as the Indian advanced, his hands wrapped around the barrel of the rifle.

"It is good. It had to come to this, tall one. You and I," the stony face said. Red Claw swung the rifle as a club, a powerful, short swing that Fargo easily avoided.

He let Red Claw come forward again, waited, poised on the balls of his feet. The Indian swung the rifle again, a longer sweep this time. The heavy stock of the rifle whistled past his face and Fargo moved with the speed of a cougar's leap, his hands shooting out and upward to close around the gun. He twisted, putting all the strength of his shoulder muscles in it. But Red Claw let go of the rifle and Fargo felt himself fall off-balance from the force of his twisting motion. He landed on one knee and knew he'd been tricked, twisted his head away, but the blow still came down hard along the back of the neck. He fell forward, tried to roll away, but the Arapaho was both quick and powerful and Fargo grunted in pain as the kick landed hard into the small of his back. Again, he pitched forward and felt the Indian's arms wrap around his

155

neck. With long arms, Red Claw yanked Fargo's head upward and got both arms around his foe's neck. He squeezed and Fargo felt his breath start to cut off. He had only a few seconds, he realized, and the bronzed arms were locked tight around his neck.

He used all the strength of his powerful thigh muscles to push himself upward and he carried the Indian along with him. But Red Claw's grip stayed locked and Fargo spun his body around, used up his last few moments of precious breath to whirl in a circle as though he were doing a wild dance, and still the Indian clung to him. With a last whirl, Fargo flung himself onto his back, all his weight landing on top of the Arapaho. He heard the man's grunt and the grip around his neck loosened for an instant. But an instant was all he needed and he tore free, rolled, and came up on his feet, hearing the sound of his rasping breath as he drew in great gulps of air.

But Red Claw moved at him again, the stone face holding only the hint of a snarl, and this time he held a hunting knife in his hand. Fargo drew the empty Colt from its holster and pulled back to avoid a swiping blow. Red Claw struck again, another long swipe, then a lunge and another lunge. He used the knife with practiced dexterity and each blow brought him inches closer to his target. Fargo waited, watched the Indian's wrists, and saw another lunging blow as it started. He pulled to the side and brought the Colt around in what seemed a blow at the Indian's head. But Red Claw easily pulled away with an agile step. Fargo came in with another attempt and again the Arapaho easily avoided it.

Red Claw lunged again with the knife, a quick, sharp blow that grazed Fargo's shoulder, and he easily avoided the answering swipe Fargo gave with the six-gun. In the black-coal eyes, Fargo caught the glint of contempt and took a grim satisfaction in it. He moved tentatively, watched the Indian's wrist, and once again Red Claw lunged, a sharp, lightning-fast lunge, and Fargo felt the knife tear through the side of his shirt. But this time he brought the Colt around in a smashing, quick arc, no ineffective blow aimed at the Indian's head but a smash that brought the barrel of the gun full on Red Claw's hand. The Arapaho uttered a grunt of pain as the knife fell from his momentarily numbed fingerrs.

Fargo leaned down, swept the knife from the ground just as Red Claw leaped forward with a roar of rage. The Arapaho chief, both feet off the ground, made a diving leap just as Fargo brought the knife up. His broad chest impaled itself on the blade and Fargo heard the crunching sound of bone being splintered as the Indian's full weight came down on the knife. Fargo stepped back as he let go of the handle of the knife and watched Red Claw fall forward with a hissing sound. The Arapaho landed on the ground and drove the knife still further into his chest, rolled onto his back, shuddered, uttered a final hissing sound, and lay still. The black-coal eyes stared lifelessly up at the big man that stood over him.

"No more hostages. No more anything," Fargo spat. He holstered the Colt and walked away to where the pony had halted, climbed on, and rode back. The still-smoking, charred remains of the compound came in sight and he saw the crowd gathered outside. Some of the troopers were loading the slain Arapahos into a big flatbed dray with stake sides. Titus detached himself from the crowd and Fargo saw he was leading the Ovaro.

"I think you're on the horse, sonny." Titus grinned.

"Believe you're right, old-timer," Fargo said as he slid to the ground. He grasped the hand Titus Toomey extended to him.

"Good work, young feller," Titus said. "Real good work. I saw you go after Red Claw. He give you trouble?"

"More than I wanted," Fargo said. He saw the lieutenant limp forward and smile. "You did real well," Fargo told him.

"Thank you, sir," Baker said with military respect.

"What do you do now?" Fargo asked.

"We'll stay here in a field camp. I'll send a report to headquarters and in time they'll get a crew out to rebuild the compound," the lieutenant said.

Fargo nodded and let his gaze move over the crowd that was beginning to head back into town. He saw Molly with Emily and Ed Kroger and she came forward to stop before him. "I'm sorry about that night, Fargo," she said.

"That makes two of us," he said coldly. She turned away and slowly rejoined the Krogers. He swept the others again and finally saw the honey-wheat hair coming toward him. Bess carried her two traveling bags and set them down in front of him.

"Lieutenant Baker said he'd give me a packhorse for my bags," she said.

"Going home?" Fargo asked.

"In time," she said.

"Where else?" he queried.

"Wherever you're going," she said with matter-of-factness. She reached up and pressed her mouth to his. "Any objections?" she murmured.

"Not a one," he said. "Not a one."

LOOKING FORWARD!

**The following is the opening
section from the next novel in the exciting
Trailsman series from Signet:**

THE TRAILSMAN #71
RENEGADE REBELLION

*1860, the Oklahoma Territory just above the
Kiamichi River, where respectability and
savagery hid behind the same mask . . .*

They were a lynching party. He'd seen enough of
them to know at once. Only there was a difference.
Not in type or attitude. That was usual enough. Six of
them rode, raw-faced and calloused, men who enjoyed
lynching, taking coarse glee in their anticipation. Their
victim rode in the center and that was typical. Wrists
tied behind the back. That was the same too. But
there the usual abruptly ended. No burly cowhand sat
in tight-lipped defeat. No rangy horse thief rode with
head bowed in guilty resignation. This victim was a
slender figure in a dark green blouse and skirt to
match, high breasts bouncing in unison with her mount's
stride, her medium brown hair swept up and back
from her forehead and held atop her head with a
tortoise shell clip.

Fargo moved through the thick stand of horse chestnut until he was almost parallel to the riders. He'd just wakened and breakfasted in the cool shade of the forest when he heard the horses nearing at a gallop. He had the Colt in hand as they appeared beyond the foliage along an open stretch of ground and he had frowned at once. He never like lynching parties, most self-serving and all aimed at shortcutting the law. Hanging was one thing, lynching another.

He'd swung onto the Ovaro and sent the magnificent black and white horse through the trees as he followed the riders and now he reined to a halt as they came to a stop. The girl was young, with a pert, pugnacious face, a small upturned nose, and round cheeks, he took note. If she was afraid, she didn't show it. Anger and defiance held her face and he saw medium brown eyes flash at the men that surrounded her.

"This'll do," the front rider said, and indicated a buckeye with a long, low branch made for a lynch rope. He dismounted, a thin-faced man with thin lips, then reached up and pulled the girl from the saddle.

"Bastards," she snapped as she hit the ground.

"We ain't gonna let all that go to waste, are we, Hawks?" one of the others said out of thick lips and a puffy face.

The man called Hawks frowned. "Meanin' what?"

"We might as well enjoy her, first," the other one said. "The boss ain't gonna care any."

"Guess not," Hawks said, and the others left their saddles to gather around the girl. "Me first, though," Hawks announced.

"Bastards," she hissed. "I didn't do it, damn you."

"You were seen, by more than enough folks," another man chimed in.

"Dooley saw you," the beefy-faced man said.

"He does nothing but lie and cheat in that card palace of his. He'd do the same anywhere," she snapped.

"Polly saw you," Hawks snarled.

"It wasn't me she saw," the girl shouted.

"And Cyril Dandridge saw you hightailing it down the road. Everybody knows that dark red cape you wear," Hawks added.

"It was stolen a few days ago. I never knew it was missing," she said. She held to her story, Fargo observed. But then she'd have to do that much, he realized.

"Cut the damn talk and let's get a piece of her lyin' little ass," one of the others interrupted.

The thin-faced man closed his hand around the neck of the girl's blouse. "You better enjoy this, bitch, because it's going to be your last screw in this world." He laughed harshly.

"Go to hell," the girl flung back.

"Untie her wrists so's we can get her clothes off. I like my piece soft and naked when I get it." The man with the beefy face chortled.

"Just tear them off, dammit," another shouted impatiently. Fargo's eyes swept the six men as they crowded around. His eyes took in the way each of them moved, the hang of their arms, and the cut of their bodies and he glanced at their hands and the six-guns on their gunbelts.

"Wait," he heard the girl say, and returned his eyes to her. "I guess there's nothing else but to enjoy it if it's going to be my last time," she said.

"Count on it, tramp," Hawks growled.

"Then untie my hands and I'll make you enjoy it more," she said, and Fargo felt the frown press itself across his brow and he peered at the girl. She suddenly seemed resigned, an instant change in her that surprised him.

"Untie her," Hawks barked, and one of the others used a knife to slit the ropes holding her wrists. The girl brought her hands in front of her as she rubbed circulation back into her wrists. Slowly, she began to unbutton the blouse as Hawks waited in front of her, his eyes widening with anticipation. The others backed a few paces as they shifted their feet in coarse glee.

"This'll go quicker if you help," she said to Hawks, and the man stepped close to her and began to undo the lower buttons. Fargo stared at the girl and felt the surprise still pushing at him when she suddenly exploded into action, her hand snapping out with the quickness of a young cat to close around the six-gun in the man's holster. She yanked it out in one lightning motion but she had to take precious seconds to turn the gun in her hand and Hawk had the chance to fling himself away from her. But the shot caught him high on the shoulder and he let out a cry of pain as he fell back.

Two of the nearest men rushed at her as she whirled and brought the six-gun around to fire again. She got off another shot that grazed the temple of the beefy-faced one. "I'll take at least one of you with me, you rotten bastards," she screamed, fired again but with too much haste as the third man ducked, came in low, and tackled her around the knees. She went down as she fired a wild shot before the others closed in on her. She fought with the fury of a cornered wildcat as they grabbed at her, and Fargo saw her legs kicking out, her hands trying to rake their faces with her nails. But they took hold of her finally, Fargo saw as they yanked her to her feet. One of them smashed his hand across her face but drew only a curse from her.

"String her goddamn neck up," Hawks shouted, and Fargo saw him pressing a kerchief to his shoulder. "Just kill her." The others obeyed and began to drag the girl to the tree where one quickly looped the rope across the low, thick branch. Fargo sent the Ovaro into a fast trot while he was still in the trees and emerged into the open less than a dozen yards from the men and saw them hold on to the girl as they turned in surprise to stare at him.

"Party's over, gents," he said almost affably.

"Who the hell are you?" Hawks snapped.

"Delegate from the antilynching society," Fargo said. "Just let the girl go and we'll all stay friendly."

"The hell we will, mister. Get your ass out of here or we'll make it a double." Hawks pressed the kerchief harder against his shoulder.

"That so?" Fargo smiled, his hand resting on the butt of the big Colt at his hip. "I think I'll turn that down. So will the young lady. Now just let her go."

"She's a goddamn murdering bitch," one of the others shouted.

"The law call her that yet?" Fargo inquired.

"We don't need to wait for the law. We know and lynchin's too good for her," Hawks snarled.

"They're following orders, that's all," the girl snapped.

"She killed the finest man in town," one of the others said, a big, burly man with small eyes, avoiding the girl's accusation.

"We'll let the law decide that," Fargo said.

"I'll tell you one more time, mister. You ride fast or you're a dead man," Hawks rasped.

"Hang 'em both," one of the others put in.

"Can't ride off," Fargo said calmly.

"Why the hell not?" Hawks bit out.

"Against my principles. Got a prejudice against lynchings."

The one with the beefy face stared at the big man on the Ovaro. "You must be loco, mister. There are six of us," he said.

"Damn," Fargo swore. "My mama always told me to learn to count." He saw them exchange quick glances suddenly filled with uncertainty about this big, handsome man who faced them with unruffled calm. Fargo smiled inwardly. That would make their moves even more nervous and unsteady and he surveyed the group again. Hawks was already no threat with his injured shoulder. The two men to his right, Fargo had already noted, were slow moving and clumsy. Their gun hands wouldn't be any faster. That left three standing alongside each other, two that might be of average quickness and the third, the burly figure, had thick-fingered, heavy hands more able to wield a smithy's tongs than a six-gun.

He waited and watched the uncertain glances harden. Like most men with more surface conceit than real courage, they had to prove themselves in front of each other and he expected that too. As the two on his left started to draw their guns, he had the big Colt out of its holster and in his hand with one smooth, lightning-fast motion. The two shots sounded almost as one and the two men collapsed in a heap against each other, one with blood spreading from his chest, the other with his abdomen gushing. Fargo swung the Colt as the two slow-moving figures at his right had just cleared their holsters. He fired again and the two figures went down as though poleaxed. Fargo brought the Colt around and saw the thick-fingered man drop back, fear on his face as he kept his hand away from his holster. Hawks started to move for his gun, winced, and thought better of the idea.

"Drop your gunbelts, nice and slow," Fargo said, and the two men carefully complied. "Get on your horse, honey," Fargo said to the girl, and watched her pull herself onto the mount with a flash of sturdy, well-turned calf. "Walk your horse next to me," he told her. He turned as she came alongside and began to walk the Ovaro very slowly but his wild-creature hearing was tuned to the two figures he'd left standing behind him. He caught the faint sound the moment it came and cursed inwardly, the soft slurred sound of leather suddenly creasing, the sliding hiss of a gun being pulled from its holster. Fargo whirled in the saddle, the Colt steadied against his abdomen.

It was the burly thick-fingered man, crouched on the ground with the gun just drawn out of the gunbelt he'd dropped. Fargo fired as the man raised his six-gun and the burly figure catapulted backward, straightened out in midair, and dropped flat onto its back. The man lay still except for a last gurgling sound that sent tiny bubbles of red from his lips. "Damnfool," Fargo murmured, and his gaze bored into Hawk. The man pulled backward and slumped to one knee, only abject fear in his face.

"I won't try anything, honest, mister," he pleaded.

"Ride," Fargo said to the girl, and sent the Ovaro into a trot. He rode back into the horse chestnuts, following a deer path through the forest until he finally emerged onto a cleared slope where a stream bubbled its way downhill. He halted, swung to the ground, and watched the girl pull up and dismount. As the horses made for the stream, he took her in more carefully and saw medium brown eyes blink at him out of her pertly pretty face. But a tiny furrow touched her brow beneath the upswept hair and she regarded him with a mixture of gratefulness, curiosity, and wariness.

"Why'd you do it?" she asked. "I'm grateful to you. Good God, I am. But why? You could've got yourself killed."

"Didn't expect that to happen." Fargo smiled and watched her regard him with her brown eyes narrowed.

"Guess not, seeing the way you handled that Colt," she said. "But why? You could've gone your way. Most would have."

Fargo shrugged. "Don't like lynch parties. Never have."

"Then I'm grateful for that too," she said. "Saying thank you doesn't sound near enough for having saved my neck, but I've no other words for it."

"They'll do," Fargo said. "You've a name?"

"Clover," she answered. "Clover Corrigan." Her eyes waited.

"Fargo, Skye Fargo. Some call me the Trailsman," he answered. "Now you want to tell me your side of this, Clover Corrigan?"

She turned away for a moment and stared into space. She had a neat, solid figure and high breasts, a round, sturdy shape with curves in the right place but everything put together compactly. "I can't tell you much of anything," she said.

"Who was it they said you killed, the one they called the finest man in town?"

"Douglas Tremayne," she said.

"You knew him well?" Fargo asked, his eyes peering sharply at her.

"I worked for him," she said. "But I didn't kill him."

"Sounds like he was found dead and you were seen hightailing it," Fargo said.

"It wasn't me," she snapped angrily as he searched her face for the slightest sign of hesitation or slyness. But the only thing he saw flash in her pert face was anger and indignation.

"What about that dark red cape they said you wore?" Fargo pressed.

"I didn't even know it was missing. Somebody took it to set me up."

"Why?"

"I don't know, dammit," she said, and Fargo saw the frown dig harder into her smooth brow as she stared back. "You don't believe me, do you?" she said accusingly, with a touch of hurt in her voice. She was either very clever or very innocent, he decided.

"I didn't say I didn't believe you," he answered.

"You as much as said it. Do you or don't you?" she insisted.

"Can't say," he answered honestly, and saw the instant anger flare in her brown eyes.

"Then you're the same as they were," she snapped.

"I'm not trying to lynch you," Fargo said quietly. She took in his answer with a glower. "You're asking me to just up and believe you. You've no right to ask that."

"Why not? I didn't do it."

"I've been fooled by words before. Pretty faces too. Believing takes more."

"I haven't got more, not now," she said. "If I'd time, maybe I could find out more. I have to."

Fargo let his lips purse. She had an angry directness that held no guile in it. But, he reminded himself again, some women were mighty fine actresses. "You saying I should just let you go your way," he remarked.

"Yes, so's I can find the truth of it," she said.

"Or head for Texas," Fargo said, and she flared at once.

"You're making it awful hard to stay grateful," she threw at him.

"Let's ride and I'll listen some more. There's got to be more you can tell me, maybe more than you know there is," he said. She shrugged as the glower remained and climbed onto her horse with a quick, angry motion that made her high, round breasts bounce. Fargo began to lead a slow pace along the slope and kept his questions calmly casual. "I passed through Two Forks Corners a day ago. I take it this all happened back there," he said.

"Just outside of town, at Douglas Tremayne's house."

"Tell me about him."

"He was the town banker, leading citizen, popular with everybody. He was handsome, smooth, about forty but looked thirty."

"What'd Clover Corrigan do for him?" Fargo questioned.

"He hired me about a year ago. I helped him with whatever he needed, from making coffee, filling in as clerk at the bank, seeing to his appointments, to cleaning up his house. Sometimes he'd keep me late into the night writing down thoughts he had for a speech he was to make. Sometimes I'd fix dinner for him. I was part assistant, part maid."

"Anything else?" Fargo asked.

"No, nothing else," she snapped angrily. "I know that a lot of people thought that but it wasn't true. Douglas Tremayne and I were never really close. For all the things he had me do for him, none of it was ever anything real important. I never did really know him. I always felt that."

Fargo watched the troubled frown wreathe her pertly pretty face. For all her anger and glower she had a lostness to her that reached out. She rode alongside him completely unaware that he had made a wide circle back toward Two Forks Corners. "Who were those men that wanted to string you up?" he asked.

"Hawks is a two-bit horse trader that Douglas Tremayne lent money to when no one else would. Ahern, the big one, was the town smith and drunk. Douglas kept him in business too, just as he did with the others. Hell, the whole town would've been with them by afternoon. Douglas Tremayne was everybody's friend. He sure wasn't the average banker," Clover said.

"Where'd they get to you?" Fargo asked.

"Came to my place. I'd just finished dressing when they dragged me out. I'd been home all night but they wouldn't believe it and I couldn't prove it," she said.

"Not with all the folks that saw you running," Fargo commented.

"Not me, dammit. They didn't see me," Clover exploded.

"You got any ideas who they saw?" he asked, and watched her closely as she frowned in thought.

"No, not yet," she said slowly. "In that cape of mine, it could've been anybody, even a man."

"I suppose so," Fargo thought aloud. "Tremayne have a girlfriend?"

"I can't say for sure but I suspected he did. Once I found a blue slipper with a red bow in his closet, like someone forgot to pack it away before leaving in a hurry. As I said, for all I did for him, there was a lot about him I never got to know."

Fargo pulled up as they finished the full circle and let the Ovaro graze on a patch of sweetclover. Two Forks Corners lay north, just beyond a thick stand of cottonwoods. All the time they'd talked, he'd watched her and had seen no sign of glibness or guile. But he saw her watching him, picking up the thoughts that moved across his mind. "You've done a lot of asking and you're thinking all you've got is more words," she said.

He smiled wryly. "That's right."

"Because I can't give you more yet," she flared. "I've got to find out what happened myself."

"How do you figure to do that with a whole town waiting to lynch you?" Fargo questioned.

"I don't know." She frowned. "I'll find a way. There's got to be a way, someplace to start." She halted and turned a long glance at him. "You could help me."

"I already did that," he said.

"I know and that sort of makes me your responsibility," Clover tossed back with a smugness coming across her face.

"What?"

"Well, it does. Hawks is going to tell about you and that Ovaro's easy to spot," she said. "They'll say I killed Douglas Tremayne and you helped me escape. You've got to help me."

"Damn, you've more than your share of brass," Fargo growled, and she shrugged and was suddenly quite happy with herself. But she did have hold of a kernel of fact and he didn't want more trouble. "I stopped a lynching. Nothing wrong in that," he said. "But I'll tell you what I'll do. I'm in these parts to break trail for a cattle drive down into Houston. I'm a week early. I'll help you but we'll do it my way."

She smiled, a sudden explosion of sunniness that turned her pert prettiness into warm loveliness. "I'll settle for that," she said. Something, perhaps a fleeting expression in his lake-blue eyes, caught at her and she suddenly turned a suspicious glance at him. "What's your way?" she asked.

"First, I turn you over to the sheriff in Two Forks," he said.

"Hell, you will," she exploded. "Oh, no."

"For your own protection," Fargo said.

"So you can get off the hook by turning me in and going your way," she shouted. "Forget it. You're out for yourself, just like everybody else."

"Being grateful has a short life with you, doesn't it?" Fargo said.

"Yes, when it comes to being put in jail," she snapped.

Fargo glared at her. "Damn, you're a regular little cactus," he said. "But I'm into this and I'm going to help you in spite of your suspicious, short-tempered hide. I'm taking you in."

She sat alongside him and her eyes searched his face and he saw them suddenly soften. "Maybe I am too suspicious. Maybe I should be thankful to you," she said quietly, and then her voice tightened. "But I'm not," she hissed as she smashed both hands against him.

He felt himself go sideways off the Ovaro at the unexpected force of the blow, tried to stop his fall, but his hand missed the saddle horn and he landed hard on the back of his neck. He felt the sharp pain as his head hit a rock and the world turned gray, then black, and he lay still in the sudden slumber of unconsciousness.

He hadn't any precise idea how long he'd lain there before he stirred, feeling the dull pain at the back of his head, and pulled his eyes open. He shook away fuzziness and the world took shape, the Ovaro, first, standing nearby. Fargo pushed himself to his feet, his hand automatically going to the holster. "Damn," he swore as he found only empty leather, and he peered at the horse. She'd taken the big Sharps from the saddle holster too, he saw and swore again under his breath. He pulled himself onto the Ovaro, let the last cobwebs clear from his mind, and saw the tracks where she'd turned and raced up the slope.

He started following the hoofprints and knew he wasn't at all certain whether he was following a scared, angry, brassy little package of fiery innocence or a very clever and determined pert-faced killer.